Living w

Amanda Attfield

CHELONIST

First published in Great Britain in 2012 by Chelonist Ltd

Chelonist Ltd
Knapp View
Westhope
Hereford
HR4 8BL

A CIP catalogue record for this book is available
From the British Library

ISBN 978-0-9573921-0-6

This book is a work of fiction. Names, characters,
businesses, organisations, places and events are
either the product of the author's imagination
or are used fictitiously. Any resemblance to
actual persons, living or dead, events or
locales is entirely coincidental.

I am indebted to my family for putting up with my absence, and Liz for helping with proof reading.

1. Not remembering

There was the thin line of spittle, the one I'd seen a hundred, no, many more than a hundred times before. A familiar foamy strand, like spume that washes up on the shoreline, only spume smells of the sea, seaweed, rotted sea-type stuff, seagull feathers, and sand – can sand smell? Sand has a smell. This had no smell. The spittle was usually just before. Just before. But not this time. The cup shook in my hand. Bone china. The one she had, the one she always wanted when she said,

'Where's my tea, then?'

And I would get the tea. Half a sugar, no more. Stirred. Properly, so it dissolved. It shook in my hand, the china cup. On the china saucer. The one that matched. It had to be the one that matched. I'd been there before, with one that did not match. Only this time, she was quite still. Eyes open. Usually they were open in a sort of starey sort of way, then closed, and opened again with a strain, as if she battled to wrench them open against some great force trying to keep them shut. The blood vessels stood out then on her neck, at her temples, and on her eyelids. Time slowed somehow, even though it didn't really. And then I would breathe in, and it would come. But here, this time, nothing. No blood vessels. Nothing. The face was quite still. The bedroom was half lit, one

1

curtain opened, one not. Window open, breeze waving the curtain and the nets about. She was on the bed, strangely.

'Your tea, Julia. Julia, here's your tea.'

Nothing. The teacup over balanced and fell, spilling tea on the carpet. Clumsy. There was a penalty for the clumsy and another for the mess. God. I think now that God is a woman. Definitely. Or maybe no gender, actually. Not male that's for sure because if male then seasons would not exist so that cricket, rugby, and football would be every week not just at some times in the year. I never liked those curtains. And the cup was broken on the carpet. And still there was still nothing. And I could not remember how I came to be in the bedroom, or why the saucer was in my hand, my left hand. And there was Julia on the bed with snot from her nose, and spit down her chin, and her eyes open. There was no sound. Yes - there was a sound. Bloody sparrows that had taken to the holly tree at the back of the house. Whoever said sparrows were declining was right. They were declining into our garden, which was where the whole sparrow population of England were now. But that wasn't it. No sound of Julia. Not her voice, not her deliberate intake of breath, not her breathing. No breath. Not breathing. I put down the saucer. I can't recall making the tea. Just this; that I was there in the bedroom and she was quite still. It could be a trick. To trick me to do the clumsy tea thing. I reached out my hand, slowly. She could have grabbed me. She had done that before. With a finger I touched her shoulder. I poked her shoulder with two fingers, I said,

'Julia?'

Nothing. I poked her again more roughly. I stabbed her with my two fingers. Nothing. The eyes were still open. She had a kind of odd not a smile exactly, but a smile, sort of. Many people would do the mouth-to-mouth thing. Was this a medical emergency? I'd seen that on that whatsit programme, Greys Anatomy. No thanks. It had been a long time since Julia and I did anything like that. She never liked it. She didn't like any of that. Not with me anyway. No need to start now. She looked what I could imagine was dead. She was – dead. I'd not seen a dead person before, not like this. I saw my younger brother after the accident in the chapel of rest. He was all kind of waxy, and had his hair all strange as if it wasn't his hair at all. It wasn't him. This wasn't her. Too peaceful. Julia was not peaceful.

I'd imagined this so many times in my head, how she would ask for the tea, and I would say 'Get it your damned self'. Or something like that, maybe 'Get it yourself' without the 'damned' bit. And she'd punch me in the arm and I wouldn't care, I'd grab her hand as she went to hit me and hold it, just hold it and turn it all the way back to her. I knew I was stronger. And I'd push her back, hard, and she'd fall over, look at me and see me as her husband, man of the house, and come to me crying and sorry. She

she'd say how sorry she was and how she hadn't meant to do it, any of it, and things could be different, just for me to not hit her. So was that it then? Did she call me by that name? Was that it? Was it real? I went to the bathroom and took a piss. Standing up with a bit of tissue under me, to catch the drops, so they wouldn't drop on the seat or onto the wee catcher.

'I'm sick of your nasty smelly wee stuff all over the bathroom. Can't you wee sitting down, or wipe your mess?'

Once I found the wee mat on my pillow. It was easier to give in. Just easier. And it was so quiet now. It dawned on me that I did not have to wipe the drops. I threw the tissue, guiltily, into the toilet bowl, put the toilet seat down, and let a few drops fall on the seat. What had happened? I couldn't remember. I washed my hands. Was I like Pilate? What sin was there to wash out? Or Lady Macbeth? - only she was a woman, obviously. We'd done that play at school. I may have been thick as shit, but I'd got to play Banquo. I got killed and had to come back as the ghost when they were all having dinner. They reckon Shakespeare is like real life, only lots of people got killed in Shakespeare all the time, at least they did in the plays we did. Was I like that Macbeth woman then, stained, spotted with blood?

2. Not getting married, and getting married

God she was gorgeous. Wild blonde hair, and clear blue eyes, and perfect, perfect teeth. I didn't care when I found out later that the blonde was from a bottle. It suited her, and she turned heads, my God did she. Popular, that's what she was. With unpopular me. I felt a million having her on my arm. When she agreed to meet me that first time for a drink at the Three Crowns, I couldn't believe it. Me? And she had said yes. I could see the look in the faces of the other guys. Envy. Of me. Of me! I was not exactly the catch of the neighbourhood. Good with my hands, yes, and practical. Not brainy like some I'd been at school with, who'd gone on to university and stuff. But I'd saved up and bought a derelict property, done it up while working the farm. Then moved in there, and still worked on the farm, to save up for another. All hours, all the bloody hours, God knows. Up at the crack for milking, all weathers, wind, rain, frost and such when all others are in their beds, and then to the house to sort wiring, plumbing, and plastering. Did it all myself. Night school helped. Got my City and Guilds. Couldn't see what she saw in me, really. Well, I guess she didn't see it in me, more wanted me as her rescue plan. Anyway, that came later. It was always later that you saw your fool shadow plonking along behind, while the you that was, can't believe how you could not have seen it. There was no blindness

5

like the present. I'd liked to have had those crystal clear eyes of the future, to illuminate everything for the blind fool I was then. All those early wakings up while my father snored and slept off his drink, his knuckles bruised from having hit the wall, or slapped my mother. And my mother probably crying herself to sleep each night. Bastard. He used to whack Paul, and me, with mother in between trying to keep him off us, and she'd cop it too. Left to him the farm would have gone under. As soon as I was big enough, fourteen I think, I cracked him one, and told him if he ever hit me, or my mother again, he'd answer to me. That was when I knew I had to get out. Paul, my older brother had long since left. No interest in the farm. Got himself involved with a woman who owned quite a few acres out Ledbury way, spent most of his time in Poland recruiting immigrant workers for their strawberry business, and whenever I met him crowed on and on about how much they were making, and the apple tonnage they were bringing for Bulmers. Did I know I'd probably be drinking their apples? I didn't like even cider. And he didn't even come back for my wedding. Nor Dad's funeral. Good job too as we'd only have rowed and that would have upset Mum. She never liked us arguing. By that time anyway I'd left home. It was a few years after that Dad left. Bloody emotional coward that he was, left Mum and set up home with that Janice woman that used to clean for them. That will have been Janice's doing, bitch that she was.

And she had her husband still living with her. Much that he knew that she was getting her oats in that way, as he was well older than her, and by that time was more than a sandwich or two short of a packed lunch. But God, Julia, how I was bewitched by her. I thought it love then. But it was a kind of bewitchment – if that's a word. And she would toss her shock of hair as she mounted me, and laugh, press her hands onto my chest and shoulders, and rock away with me deep inside her. She was the first. The only one I thought I would ever want. And I wanted her. I wanted her in the cowshed, in the stable, behind the runner beans and the shot cabbage, shot so high we could slide down naked in the heat of day, in the cool of night, hidden from the world. I wanted her. I wanted her so much I was worried I might break her, so small and bird like she was, like an elfin or something, like nothing I'd ever known.

'Let's get married,' I said.

'No,' she said,

'I'm not ready to get married yet.'

So we did not get married then.

I went with my neighbour, Dianne, and her two sons, to see that Lord of the Rings film. I'm not into films as a rule, and she – the neighbour – knew that, and I had got far too much else to do, but she said

'All work and no play Jack…..'

So I went.

This one did grab me. It seemed to me that I was Sauron, my one great eye fixed on Julia, her attention to me was a distraction from the real business that was going on everywhere else, she was getting ready to throw the ring in the fire – or the compost heap in her case. The distraction lasted a long time. Twelve years. I asked her to marry me after two years. I was twenty two. After buying the third house, I asked her again. She said no. She wanted to move in with me, but I wanted things right. I wanted it all proper. Mum had married dad expecting Paul, I knew that, and that was a mistake. I got a fourth house then, and was doing that up. She turned up on the doorstep one night, I was up to my elbows in plaster, and said

'Well, I guess we could get married then'.

I thought she might be pregnant, but she said it wasn't that. She said she'd thought about it, and didn't want to live with her mother, so if it was alright with me we could get married and she'd move in. So we did that. And God help me. I never knew what colour her real hair was. One minute blond, the next brunette. I didn't know why women did that. Mind there's all sorts of things that women did that were a complete mystery. Like even the way they think and stuff. You had to guess at it, like it was some kind of game, even though they knew what they were thinking and could come right out and tell you. But, no. You had to second guess it the whole time. And then get it in the neck for not guessing it right. Presents for example. The engagement ring. I was supposed to know what style she wanted. To make it a surprise. The trick was that it had to be a surprise that is not a surprise at all. The one I got was, of course, not right. Diamonds and all, and really expensive. I dug into my savings for it, specially, when I'd really rather have put them towards the fencing for the top field. Only she took it back to the shop and exchanged it for a single diamond set in white gold. And who was I to talk about what women think, having had only one woman my entire life up to then. But I had read about it. And heard Bob talk about it. Since his divorce he'd had quite a few girlfriends. He said getting divorced was the best thing he'd ever done, apart from he missed the children a lot. He came round when he heard that we'd decided to get married, and said,

'Well, so you finally got round to it. I guess we all do in the end. You sure you know what you're doing?'

He'd married Susie straight from school. It was ok for him, at least it was then. The thing was, I didn't know if I was sure or not. I said,

'Yeah, sure I'm sure, let's have a drink, eh?'

And we had a drink and talked about the cricket. He was mad keen on cricket. I could take it or leave it. I did enjoy a match or two and did go to Edgbaston with him a few times. He wanted me to go to the Windies with him next tour. I might well do that, I thought. But then, what about Julia? It did seem inevitable somehow, that Julia and I should get married. Who else was there after all? I didn't go out. Spent all my spare hours on one of the houses, or sorting tenants, or hard landscaping the garden, or fitting kitchens and stuff. There was always someone who wanted something doing, and they were prepared to pay good money. Silly money sometimes – specially the women. They did seem to like having me in the house, talking over and planning what they wanted. They seemed amazed that I could talk sensibly about kitchens and how best they needed to be laid out. I'd got three regular women clients, all of whom wanted stuff making or changing, or fixing, all the ruddy time.

So Julia and I got married at St Nicholas's. Once you fix on something like a wedding, it all rumbles along and takes you with it. I guess most people would say that. Like getting bowled along by a strong wind. You knew if you made the effort you could get out of it, duck into a corner or away, but somehow there's the weight of it, the strength gusting you along, something about letting go to a greater force, letting go and letting it all happen to you. In a weird kind of way it was restful not having to make decisions or do much. At least that's what I thought. Julia was the greater force. Even so, she would get annoyed with me for not paying more attention to the wedding plans, and accused me of not being interested at all. I wasn't really, but how could I tell her that? So I made like I was interested. I think she knew it was a pretence, but she went along with that.

Before the wedding Caroline came to see me. She was Julia's best friend. She rang up, out of the blue. She said she needed to see me, on my own, and that it was about the wedding. I did wonder about why she couldn't tell me on the phone, and pressed her on this, but she said she simply couldn't say over the phone. No chance of Julia turning up, this was her Pilates night. I was in the workshop, in the spray booth, spraying a three-drawer cabinet with its final coat. I'd done the drawers already, and was pretty pleased with how it was looking. I heard the workshop door bang shut, and Caroline call

'Jack? Jack are you in there?'

I shouted back.

'Yep, here. Gimme a minute.'

We went into the kitchen, and I made us some tea. The kettle was already warm from standing on the Aga, so it didn't take long. I asked her outright why she wanted to see me. She was standing, and she turned away, then turned back to me, looked at the floor, then at me, then away again. I could see it was hard for her to say, so I waited. We both just waited there. When things are silent it seems like ages, but it's not really, like when I walked out across the fields, and down to the stream, it would be quiet then, only the birds – magpies usually, a buzzard sometimes, or a jay, and always crows. Once it was getting on into the evening and a fox cut across right in front of me. Each walk in the quiet seemed to last forever, but it was only half an hour there and back.

In the kitchen silence, it can't have been even a minute. I remember I could hear the pond pump going, and thought I should clear out the pump in the next day or so. Mucky job that would be. Caroline said,

'I've thought long and hard about this, if I should say this to you, or not. Well, here goes. You know, the wedding. It's about the wedding. You and Julia. She's not good for you, Jack. Do you know that?'

I didn't know that, or at least I thought I didn't. I asked her,

'What are you getting at, Caroline?'

I thought for a horrible moment that she was going to say I should marry her instead, or something like that. I'd heard that sometimes women's best friends get all mithered over the friend's intended. Bit like in history when we did Henry VIII who had to marry his older brother's wife, something like that. She took a sip of tea and continued.

'She's not ………. how can I put this. She's been my friend, my best friend, for as long as I can remember, and this isn't easy for me, but you're a decent guy Jack, and you deserve better. She's my best friend, yes, and you're my best friend's fiancé. It's because of that, that I have to say what I have to say. I can't keep this from you. God, you can't be that blind, can you? Do you know what she's like, what she's really like? You know she's not exactly the most faithful person don't you? She's been seeing someone else, Jack. For a while. At the same time as you, y' know, seeing, well more than seeing.'

I couldn't believe it. Well, maybe deep down I could believe it. That was the problem. I think I knew all the time. What she wanted me for. But I wanted Julia, and wasn't that enough? She wanted me. She would put all that behind her when we got married. We'd have kids, and stuff, she'd live here, and she'd be happy. We'd be happy. I said this to Caroline.

'Jack, you can't be that much of a fool', she replied.

'People don't change. Does she love you? Has she said that? I thought I'd come here and tell you what I know because you need to know about what she's really like. She's been like this for years, seeing more than on bloke at a time, teasing them, playing one off against the other. I haven't minded till now because they've been right shits and they deserved it just as much as she did. But you don't. Jack, you're a decent bloke. Please just think about it for a minute. She's not what you think she is. If you marry her, you'll be marrying someone you've imagined, not the real Julia. You'll have to live with her, the real her, not your fantasy her.'

I was stunned then, to think that she could be right about the fantasy bit. That I had a picture of what it would be like with her here, in this house, in the kitchen, with kids – at least three – running around happy, a small horse or two in the next field maybe, for them to ride on. Julia would fix me breakfast, help in the garden. She loved horses. Did she love me? I was sure what I felt was love, but did I know what love was? Had she said the words? We could get horses. I had money from selling the houses, and the business, and much more to come. Even Paul had been sniffing round wanting to be my partner. Bloody cheek as if I would take him on as an equal. Work for me, yes, not partner. Things were on the up. I didn't want to be on my own, otherwise, what was it all for? I said,

'Caroline, I guess you maybe had to tell me what you've told me, but I know she's got male friends, and I know she makes out that she plays away sometimes, for a bit of fun, but that's all it is, friends, none of its serious. And she loves me. After we're married, she'll be here, with me. I can't believe she's seeing anyone else, not in that way, she wouldn't do that to me. Anyway, how do you know?'

'I can't say. You'll just have to accept my word for it. But if you are going to speak with her, ask her about Pete, from Solihull. And he's not the only one. Good luck Jack, and don't say I didn't warn you. If you ever want to talk about stuff, you've got my number. I won't speak about this again unless you want to.'

With that she got up to leave, and seemed to ignore my question about what more she knew. It was if she hadn't heard me at all but as she walked out of the kitchen, she turned to me and said that she'd said enough, probably too much, probably she should not have said anything at all, she was only trying to help me, and something about divided loyalties.

I went for the eternal walk, that this time lasted a lot longer than half an hour. I stopped for an age on the small bridge over the brook, looking down, watching its brackish water rush along and away and I wished I was like that water to rush away over all the troubled, uneven bottom, to carry along whatever fell or swam inside me, to fill up fit to bust with storm rain and field run off, to trickle along in drought, to be constant, to be let be. Maybe I was better off on my own. Or with someone else. But who else? I didn't know anyone else. Was it really so bad? Could I believe Caroline? Maybe she was just jealous. And who's this Pete? Julia had mentioned a Pete. The brook ran noisily over the stones beneath my feet. In the quiet I could always think things through.

Pete. Peter. One of the scuba guys. Was he from Solihull? She liked diving. Had done it for a few years now, on and off at weekends and such. Peter - Pete. Yes. Scuba Pete. Diving buddy. Just friends. Maybe. Maybe that's what was behind Bob's question. Maybe. Lots of maybe's. But then, there always are. I wished people, relationships, were like cabinet-making. No maybes. Measure twice, cut once. And that's the finished thing, or on the way to it. You knew where you were with wood. I had this latest piece to complete. I couldn't think about all this as well. None of it made sense. I'd finish the piece first, and then think about what to do about Julia. Tomorrow, or the day after. Maybe.

When I got home I poured myself a whisky. I did not usually drink mid-week. I needed my head for the workshop. But I needed a drink. I didn't buy whisky either, usually. People gave it me, as thank you's for this and that. And wine. Like the vicar. Gave me the Lagavullin for fixing up the church shelter. Fancy a vicar giving me whisky. And good whisky at that. The neighbours had told him I liked a drop now and then. Which was true. I never did ask Julia about Pete, or anyone, or any of it. I guess I didn't want to know about anything that would mean the end of things. Better the devil you know kind of thing. Pushed it to the back of my mind. I didn't see Caroline again until the wedding day. She was maid of honour. Some honour in all that.

3. *What I did remember*

What I did remember was coming back in from the workshop. I had finished the bookshelves early. Finally, after a lot of to-ing and fro-ing, and the changed minds and the indecision over the wood, and the finish – hers not mine – they were ready to go to Overbury Hall and be fitted into place. Then what? Then standing in the bedroom with the tea. And Julia's eyes looking out at nothing. Not the usual glare at me. Nothing. So the thing was, what had happened? They say that amnesia can overtake someone in trauma. And Julia's friend, Caroline, had done that counselling thing and I remember she had said one time about power, about women and men being equally to blame. That loads of victims were men. It wasn't just women. But then she had had a lot of red wine at the time. I think she was fishing. It made me curious to know why she had said that. She was nice, lovely in fact, not at all like Julia. And I tried to get myself up on the internet so I could find out a bit more but couldn't do it so had to call Bob over. He wanted to know why I wanted to get connected up as I was so useless with information technology. On line dating was it? Cheeky bugger. Just because Julia was touting herself all over didn't mean I was about to. That bloody Pete guy, turned out she had been seeing him years ago doing a diving course in Solihull, and he arrived round here for some reason, and it'd all started it all up again.

So, women are capable of beating up men as well as being beaten up by men. So whoopee. What's new. Takes a masters degree in bloody whatnot to work that out does it, Mr Whoever of bloody Queen Mary and Westfield College. Battered husband syndrome. That's what they call it. They don't say anything about the non-violent bit. One word would be enough to send me quietly raging. Jacky. That's what she called me. Not Jack but Jacky, to taunt me. And what about finding your wife in the hay barn, legs wrapped round lover boy – what about that. And then another picking her up at the house as bold as you like. I couldn't say anything to Bob, about that obviously. Wouldn't want to. Even though it was pretty clear what was going on. He knew, and I knew. I knew he knew, and he knew I knew. That was enough.

Julia said being married to me was 'frustrating as hell', and that I was 'rubbish in bed', that she may as well be married to a girl – Jacky, she called me – she had to get satisfaction somehow, and if her husband couldn't do it for her, then she had to go elsewhere. She kept on about 'inadequate'. My fault then. Another thing I just couldn't guess. I was tired. Very tired. Happy in the workshop, but ready to drop when I'd done. She liked the money alright. From the word go. I remember when we flew off on honeymoon how she'd ordered champagne for us on the plane. When we arrived in the hotel she argued with the reception about not having had the courtesy chocolates and champagne that newlyweds were entitled to. It was the first time I'd been abroad. It seemed fine to me, too hot, and too sunny and too dry, but fine otherwise. We met a couple on the plane, bit younger than us. Julia said she thought them common and didn't want to mix with them. I thought they were good company. Each night after dinner we'd meet up at the bar and chat over a bottle of local wine, then have liqueurs and such. He was into jewellery, knew a lot about gold and diamonds, watches, and the like. Also, strangely, engineering. Said he was an engineer by trade and the jewel stuff was just a hobby that had got a bit serious. She was a fitness instructor at a local gym not too far from us as it turned out. Julia was only interested when he told us he had done some diving. He told us about when he lost a massive gold bracelet when diving in the Red Sea, off Hurghada, and it being found, amazingly, by another diver and they played a trick on him and didn't tell him until they thought he had suffered enough, then gave it back to him. Why he wore it diving I don't know. Guess he was a bit of a show off. They were thinking to emigrate to Australia and make the jewellery thing a business. I was quite interested in it all, as I'd got a bit of money I could invest in a small business, and why not Australia? What their names were now, I couldn't say, it was a long time back. Anyhow, Julia didn't speak to me for speaking with them so much, and the physical was non-existent. She said it was the wrong time. Not even on our first night of being married. It was like the tap had been turned off, or the gas down, or whatever. She gave me the total cold shoulder. I didn't try to talk to her. I needed to think. I needed the deep long eternal think of the walk across the fields. I couldn't figure out what on earth was going on. I was somewhere else in the world, in a something else marriage with someone I didn't recognise or understand. I hated these other countries. To myself, I longed for home.

In our room the walls seemed thin (along with electrics that flickered, and plumbing that thumped every time you turned the tap on), she said I was pitiful, inadequate. Sick. Not to touch her. That she was sick and tired of having to do everything. Why did I have to speak to every damned stranger and now we were stuck with those people. I was useless, she said. She'd had horses put down who could do more. I made to move towards her, to calm her down. I wondered if it was that time of the month. It was then that she punched me. Punched me. Did I do that? Did I punch her? Not then, that's for sure. I did not lay a hand on her on honeymoon. That I know for sure. She punched me, then kicked at me, slapped me across the face. I was taller than her by some way, and broader. Six foot one of me, five foot four of her. I had strong arms from the farming, and working in the workshop. I could have laid her out. It's a fact that on average men are 45 pounds heavier than women, and 4-5 inches taller, and women have less fighting experience, so I read in the paper, which makes women victims sometimes, so it said. Hard as I try, there's no way Julia was a victim. I'm not sure I was either. At least I wasn't going to admit it. I could have laid her out, easy. But I didn't. Chose not to. The last person I hit was my father, just before he left the farm for that Janice woman. I'd gone over to borrow the spare generator. There was Mum with a black eye. I didn't ask her. Just went to find him. He was in the cowshed, unusually, with Ted Jordan, who was mucking out. Jordans had been around farms and that for donkeys years. That time of day Dad was usually in bed sleeping it off. He looked up as I walked over. I didn't say a word, just grabbed him by the shoulder and whacked him across the face with my clenched fist. His head jerked backwards and he fell away into the muck. Ted looked at me, me at him. I nodded to Ted, he nodded to me. I walked out and got Mum. She came away with me to our house then, with one small bag. And even though she did go back, that caused another problem. Julia did not like her being in our house one little bit.

I must have remembered something. Surely. Something. What before the tea, and after walking from the workshop? Jesus. Did I do that then? They said that no real man would let his wife hit him. Was I not a real man then, that I'd let her hit me? God, those questions again. I went into the bedroom and looked at her. Still there. Still with that gazey, starey look, and an expression of surprise that I'd not quite taken in before. I drew the curtain and closed the window. It had blown wide open, from not being on its catch. It was interesting to me that there were no phrases for wives beating men, like there were for men beating wives. Like, 'battered wife'. 'Battered husband' just does not have the same ring. And the jokes about 'go on, sort her out', 'show her who's boss', 'who wears the trousers in your house?'. And historical sayings like 'a woman, a dog, a hickory tree, the more you beat them, the better they be.' I thought that maybe I should invent some, but the thing was, there was nothing that made it ok that your wife punched and kicked you, or made you do stuff that plain makes you feel not a man. Like denying sex. Like not wanting to make love. Like no love. Saying she didn't love you at all. Saying she only married you to get away from her mother and because you wouldn't let her live with you, and for god's sakes why bother to get divorced. Why not just divide the house up and live separate lives? Like her wanting me to piss sitting down (the toilet paper was a compromise). Like not to put my shoes under the bed but to put them on the shoe rack in the wardrobe, like not laying my clothes on the chair, like the way I squeezed the toothpaste, peeled potatoes, shaved and left shavings in the basin and didn't rinse it, didn't put the loo paper the right way round, answered the phone stupidly because she would never say that, and a hundred thousand other things that I did just living that she could not stand. She could not stand me. She didn't just not love me, she loathed me and she made me know that every day. Every single day. That time with the kitchen knife was the scariest, even though she didn't use it, just waved it about then threw it at me. Maybe it's right about no fighting experience. I guess she could have had a good stab at killing me – I did tell Caroline that in the end – it was funny that she laughed and said was I trying to be funny, which I wasn't. But I did see that it was. She couldn't have killed me, I'm too strong for her and she must have known that. I think she just wanted to try a different way to have a go. The knife just happened to be there.

So no wonder that I wondered about it then, the quiet of her being on the bed, not moving, saying nothing. And it could be that it had been me that did it. That power Caroline had talked about was there in me, and had something in me snapped. And what now? The strange thing was, I didn't care. Not one bit. It wasn't that I was glad she was dead. I didn't feel anything about her being dead. Not glad, not sad, - well, nothing really. Neutral. Dead or alive. I didn't care. And then it struck me, actually, would anyone actually care?

4. Visitors

So, there were a few times when me and Julia were really happy, or at least it seemed so. Was it like that with most folks? That it all seems happy, but it's not really, everyone going around pretending, and all the time underneath in their real lives, it's hell. But I did believe it at the time, that we had happy times, like when Bob and Sharon came over, before they were divorced of course. At least we seemed happy or pretended as such. Not deliberately, it just seemed to fall out that way, that we had friends over. I'd cook and she'd act the lady of the house. We sealed up the cracks and made it all look good as new. It was bollocks. Just a pretence. Time does funny things to memory that way. Bob would say to me,

'By heck you're a lucky bugger ain't you? What a body on that. Can't think what she saw in you.'

And then he'd get onto the cricket or some such, or what tools I'd got lately, or how was the new generator working out. I showed him my sit-on lawn mower one time, and we rode round on that a while, both a bit drunk, which I paid for later. Not physical that time, but silence, the silent stare, me saying,

'What? What is it?'

And her not replying, again as if I should know, and not have to ask, but just know somehow. I'm not bloody psychic. Then the silent stare and her jaw set, and that would be that. Silence. Sometimes for days. I'd find my Farmers Weeklies in the bin - not the recycling, which she said was a sodding nuisance and what did it matter 'cause she we would be dead anyway, and she agreed with that Jeremy Clarkson and would drive her gas guzzling four by four if she wanted it was her right, she'd earned it, and sod the save-the-planet-sandal-wearing muesli-bloody-eating-bio-organic sodding nutters. She also liked to pour my whisky away, whole bottles of it, and would do that or some other such silent punishment.

I looked up inadequate in the dictionary. It didn't have the meaning, so I looked up adequate instead. The dictionary is full of positives that way. The negative of something wasn't listed, but Julia would know it, know how to state things in the negative. When did it happen, I wondered, this seeing her negative? It had not been like that to start, it just came to be like that. No beginning, no middle, no end. Just was like that, as if it had always been like that with flashes of not like that in-between. Adequate means sufficient. So, in her world, I was not sufficient. Not that I was not able, but just not enough. Hands too rough, too fast, too slow, too soon, too late, too awkward, too heavy. Too any old reason. Not there, here. Not here, the other place, over a bit, oh God don't bother. Not sufficient. That's what Caroline had tried to get me to understand. I was thick as shit sometimes.

Julia talked sometimes about her dad, who used to visit her bedroom sometimes. Strange that that's how she put it. He used to 'visit me'. She did not say much more and me too stupid and dazed by her to find out more, and it was the early days when we first started going together. There were some things you just don't ask, then when you do, it's too late because you should have asked before and should know now. And that's when new people find out more than you do, because they ask, because they can ask. She said one or two small things, about him touching her and that she shouldn't tell her Mum about it. That it was a long time ago she said, and she had buried it, forgotten about it. Spat on her dad's grave, Caroline told me. Bastard. You heard about it on the radio, and TV, Jeremy Vine and stuff, how grownups – family mostly – did that sort of thing and worse, like make kids drink bleach. How them folks could do law and that and not have it screw them all up inside from listening to all those things, I didn't know. Caroline told me that when she did the counselling stuff, it was what she called 'boundaries'. Caroline knew stuff. I guessed it must be like having fences inside their brains to stop it running all over, except when someone scores a six. Like my electric fences to stop the foxes, and the Larsen trap. Nothing got out of that. Funny how listening in the moment is turned on or off, and when you looked back the listening is suddenly full on, volume full up and the noise of the alarm is deafening. And it all suddenly made sense. My head hurt. Bells, ringing. But it wasn't a noisy alarm from the past, it was the doorbell, the real here and now, a loud ringing chosen from a hundred front door bell tunes, followed by a voice, a loud, cheery voice.

'Hello? Hello in the house? Where are you, Jack? Are y'in y'bugger? D'y' not care who's in the house or what? I could be a burglar! Jack?'

Bob. God. I wasn't sure at all what possessed me. But I shouted down the stairs,

'Hiya. There in a min. Hang on, Bob.'

It occurred to me that no bugger much cared about Julia, and who would miss her. Really, who? What use was she to anyone, really? She was a bloody needy parasite. Her horses needed her, sure, but any fool could do that. And her not being here, what did it matter? She had been on and on recently about going on holiday to Turkey. I could send her there, sort of, not really, obviously, but pretend. No one would know. Who would know, who? Caroline was the main problem, and Julia's mother. All this in the time it took me to get to the bottom of the stairs, and by the bottom tread I had it more or less worked out. She'd go to Turkey, find 'adequate' there in the shape of however many Turkish lovers, and never come back. At least I could send her there for a holiday, while I worked out how she would never come back.

'You're a trusting bloody sod', he said to me,

'I keep telling you not to leave the door open. What if you were in the workshop? Any road, I guess Julia'd see them off, bloody scary Rottweiler that she is, eh?'

He laughed at his own joke and carried on in front of me to the kitchen.

'Bloody South Africans. That's the last time I go there on safari. What bucket of talent is it that they are supposed to have that they're just not showing at the moment? Bloody Duncan Fletcher good riddance to him. I'd have Goughie now as the England coach, yes I would. Bloody Hell I don't know. God I'm depressed. Susie's taken the kids to Cornwall for three weeks to see her mother. God I miss them. Not her obviously. What about a blow out? What d'y say? And can I borrow your sash clamps? I've got a bit of restoration work to do on an old Victorian place near Little Marcle.'

He said all this while helping himself to two beers from our fridge, opening them and passing one to me. I wasn't really listening. I was thinking about Turkey, and if I could do it. Could I do it? And I would be the left behind, wounded husband. What's the word they use on those fancy films – cuckold. Inadequate bunch of tossers. And to say the England team has talent. Was I really? Sexually I didn't really know much apart from what I did with Julia. I thought all marriages were like that. No wonder we were all so bloody miserable. But it's not what Bob's said since he'd had that one girlfriend, tantric summat or other. Like Sting he said. Sex like a pop star. Mind he was a mucky bugger, Bob. The thought struck me then. I could do it, not the sex thing, but the being without Julia thing. Getting rid of her. Yes. In my head, as a plan, but what about the body? I took a swig of beer, and thought about taking Bob into the plan. I said,

'Yes, of course you can borrow the sash clamps, I'll just get "em, they're only in the shed.'

I needed some time to think but he followed me, yattering on about how the girls were doing so well at school and didn't I think it a shame that Julia hadn't sprogged but he could see why - exclusion zone round her knickers except for everyone in the military and all sporty types of course no offence mate. (Thanks Bob). And bloody hell had I seen that dickhead the green one from Upend Lane - up your arse end lane more like - that he'd done the conversion for, had put up in the local election and no bloody way was he voting for him for the parish council, total useless tosser that he was. I gave Bob the sash clamps and decided against telling him about Julia being dead in our bedroom, and the plan to make her go away to Turkey and be adequate within her (dead) exclusion zone with all the sporty and military Turkish men. Bob sucked his beer dry, and said,

'Ta very much, mate, I'll call you about the piss up Tuesday,'

and he left, whistling. I hated whistling.

I hated people chewing as well. And when they sucked through their teeth or took a drink with a mouth full of food, and that American thing where you only ever ate with a fork as if knives hadn't been invented. What did they think they were there for? Julia hadn't sprogged. Bob had reminded me of that evening, late one night when Julia had come back in from being out somewhere. I had put that all out of my mind, behind a boundary I guessed, her standing there in the living room, angry, kind of arrogant, yes arrogant, staring at me, glaring, daring me. She'd been drinking. She said she had to get fun somehow and I was no fun and no use and as for kids she'd have kids with a real man when she found one, and anyway she'd been pregnant not that I would have noticed but got rid of it because she didn't know whose it was and what was that to me anyway? She said it was her body. I could have been a dad. I could have been. That was a six. So much for visitors.

5. Bodies

When Bob had gone, I bolted up the stairs taking two at a time. I was still thinking that maybe this wasn't real, that she'd be there drying her hair or plastering her face or something. No. She was still there. I couldn't really believe it. I ran to the bathroom and retched up the beer I'd drunk. As I dried my face I looked at myself long and hard in the mirror. Same face, same grey blue eyes, same grey brown hair. What the hell had I done? Had I done it? I simply could not remember. Bitch that she was. If she'd keeled over, surely she'd have fallen flat on her face. I examined my hands. Rough and calloused from the work in the garden, and the workshop, but no cuts, no bruises, no scratches. No blood, but then I'd washed them before. I could do it though, I could make her go away. I just had to get over the Caroline thing, and her mother. The horses. Them too. And Susie maybe, Bob's ex. She hated Bob and had sort of got pally with Julia. Enemy's enemy is my friend sort of thing. I'd have to sort them out. I went back into the bedroom. She was dead. Yes. Was she? I fetched the small mirror from the bathroom and held it against her mouth like I'd seen them do in films sometimes. Nothing. I closed her eyes. She stopped staring then, forever. Then it came to me. I could tell

Caroline that she'd gone away with her mother. And tell her mother that she'd gone away with Caroline. And get Caroline to look after the horses. Caroline. And find something to tell Bob. And Susie if that came up. I'd need to be smart about it, but that was the best thing. They'd buy that. Her mother would be awkward but it could work. At least she had a mother. She was a cow to mine when she was alive. When they were both alive. I remembered when Mum had had a turn, and came to stay with us for a while. It was great. Mum did the breakfast, and meals and that, and baked stuff. She helped out with a charity and was always up to something or other to make and take there to sell to raise money. I'd come in from the workshop to find lasagne, or beef stew and dumplings readymade for me. In the morning I'd get up sometimes really early – out of habit I guess – to get stuff done in the workshop before the heat of the day, and she'd call me for breakfast. The smell of bacon frying was great. Julia would stay in bed late, usually, and only have strong black coffee that she made herself. One morning, Julia said of the blue, bold as you like, to Mum,

'Well, don't you think it's about time you were going back home?'
 And Mum said she would not stay where she was not wanted, packed her bag and went home. Julia told me Mum had just decided that herself, and it wasn't until later, when Mum had the big stroke that killed her, that she said to me how sorry she was

that she hadn't done more for me, that she'd have stayed but could see it wasn't good for Julia and me. When I quizzed her about what she meant she said Julia had told her that we both wanted her to leave, that it was ruining the marriage, but that I wouldn't say anything for fear of upsetting her. She herself, Julia, thought she should say it, and could say it, woman-to-woman sort of thing. Bloody bitch cow woman that she was. Christ alive. And Mum then had the big stroke and I wasn't there, wasn't with her, when it happened. She was found by her neighbour. Paul came to the funeral with his partner, but I knew it was only to show willing and to make himself look like the dutiful son because he thought there'd be something in the will. Lying little git that he was, he never helped Mum not once with anything. Not when she was with Dad, not when she moved out – I did all the moving stuff – and not when she was ill the first time. Mum had nothing, of course, except the house. With that sold, and dad gone, and the money sorted out – I had to do all that of course with the lawyers - there was nothing to keep me and Paul together. Not that there was much before.

As for the death thing, Julia lying there and me doing the mirror thing reminded me of that joke, and I can't recall now who told it me, or why it should have come into my head then but it did. There's these two blokes, and the one says to the other that he'd found a body lying in the next room. The other one said,

'Oh, is he dead then?'

The first one said he thought so, and the other one said,

'Don't you think you'd better make sure?'

The first one said,

'Ok then, just a minute,' and went off. There was the sound of gunshots. The first one came back and said,

'Yes, I'm quite sure.'

I knew I didn't need to make that sure with Julia. Even so, I still thought she might wake up and grab me. Spooky. The body thing was a puzzle. I couldn't leave her in the bedroom. I'd seen something on the television, that what's it programme where they re-do old murder cases, with that woman who keeps corpses in her garden to see how they decompose. And she's got bits of bodies and whole bodies inside under heat lamps and in the cold in glass cases. There was a real life guy in the States who did that too. They were right weirdos. You couldn't just get rid of bodies. They kind of speak for themselves by the way they decomposed, that's for sure. But people did disappear completely. Some bodies were never found. There was that thing I read where they found out what happened to a woman even after she was murdered and they couldn't find her body. Turned out her husband had killed her, chopped up her body, fed it into an industrial shredder, and sprayed her remains into the snow at the side of the road. The police found her finger-nails still with the nail varnish on, and bits of bone and all sorts. The husband had hired the shredder on purpose, loaded it up on the back of the snow plough he drove, and sprayed her into the snow when he went out clearing snow. The snow had been so bad, and he'd done such a good job going out and keeping the road open, that he'd been hailed as a local hero. And all the time, he'd only done it to get rid of his wife's body. And that woman who knew about flies and that. When they discovered a body in a bedroom that had been there for years, and she found out how long and when the woman had died by the types of fly and insect larvae that had been in her body. What they could do with science and that, and technology nowadays. It was not just a case of wiping the gun clean like they used to in the old days. Lots had changed like that. You think you are moving about minding your own business, and all the time leaving bits of yourself around, like a trail of breadcrumbs - only you can't see what you leave - or being caught on cameras you didn't even know were there like you see when they catch people. Those London bomber bastards, now that was a classic. All the footage they had of them. There was no privacy really. Bloody identity cards was just the last straw. Bloody government interfering in people's lives all the time, wanting to control everything we did. Bloody nanny state was right. They should leave us alone and sort out the bloody asylum seekers that was what. I wished we could just be left alone. Alone. I was alone, sort of, now.

So I couldn't leave her body where it was. It had to be moved, hidden, buried. But where, and how? And more to the point, when? It would have to be when I could be quite sure no one would see me. Next door, Dianne, she was always on the lookout but she'd just gone off to Cyprus for a bit with her boys. So that was alright. Christ, she'd want to know about Julia too. They weren't friendly at all, but she knew about all sorts that went on in the lane and I'd have to have a story ready for her. God, that reminded me. Since her divorce she'd been extra friendly to me. The pictures thing, for example. If she knew Julia had left me for good, I reckoned she might see it as a way in kind of thing, with me, maybe. I'd noticed she was showing more of her cleavage these days, and bending over and the like when she saw me coming. Even I wasn't that thick, no matter what Julia said. I did recognise a come on. She was a bit tasty but a bit well built for me. Bob had it right when he said he'd have a go himself, only it would be like banging a bloody great lumpy pillow. Well, I'd have to cross that one if it came. As for the when, I'd need to do it soon, today? Now? Where to put her was another problem. I went to the kitchen, got another beer and went into the conservatory. As I leant on the windowsill looking out into the garden, it came to me. The compost heap. Brilliant. It was staring me in the face. At the end of the garden, I had a large compost heap. She could go in there. I wouldn't need any of it for a year or more. She would make herself useful in death in a way she never did in life. There was a word for it – irony – yes that was the word. She hated the garden, the vegetable plot, and hated the time I spent in it. She knew that it was my way of keeping out of her way. She was happy to eat the veg, though.

'Sodding useless all that,' she'd say,

'What's wrong with Waitrose? Why waste your time out there? God you're boring aren't ya, eh? All them little seeds in them little packets,' and she'd waggle her little finger at me, as if to make a point about my virility.

'Who bloody cares if it's an F1 whatever, and what does it matter what leek or cabbage it is, eh? No one cares, and it's pointless when you can just buy it.'

And she had thrown the engagement ring into the heap once, and then the wedding ring.

'You think more of that bloody heap that you do of me,'

she'd said. The thing was, I might have been dazzled by her at first, but she was right. I should never have got married. It had seemed like the right thing to do. And once married, I couldn't see how to make it otherwise. Every day, I loved her less and less like that Kaiser song that Dianne's boy played all the time at all hours, until all the love – or what I believed was love - was gone, and we were into minus. Divorce. I'd thought of that a hundred times. I didn't want her to get a penny, though. She might hate me, we might have separate bedrooms, I might hate her. She didn't want a divorce because it was easier living off me. As things stood, she wouldn't get a penny. She could bang who she liked. That was another thing. Who was she seeing that might ask questions if she disappeared? I'd have to check that out carefully with Caroline. This death / murder / cover up disappearance to never come back business was not easy, it was doing my head in a bit. There was an old green carpet in the next bedroom that I'd taken up ready to re-lay some new. I hadn't ordered the new yet. I could roll her up in that so that just in case anyone should see me taking a body to the compost, they'd think it was green stuff, not a body. Should I leave her clothes on, or not? Not. Thinking about clothes made me realise that I'd have to pack a load of stuff, make it look like she'd packed and gone. I could put the clothes in bags, and take them to the clothes bank. I should make a list. I got a pencil and some note paper. The list looked like this:

•Remove clothes

•Body in carpet

•Dig out compost heap

•Carpet and body to compost

•Bag up clothes plus more clothes

•Clothes bank

- Bottle bank
- Washing
- Food shopping
- Ring Caroline re horses

It seemed odd to look at a list with the word 'body' in it. I'd have to destroy the list as it wouldn't do if someone found it. It was hard to keep my head straight. How could I take her clothes off? It had been a long time since I saw her naked body and the thought was revolting. I felt my stomach turn over. Julia's nakedness had never been great, she looked better with clothes on, really. All skin and bone, all elbows and knees. She never ate enough. I finished the beer and went upstairs to take her clothes off. I came downstairs then because I realised I ought to dig out the compost first. I'd got them in the wrong order. Anything to put off taking off of Julia's clothes.

So I dug out the compost and bloody hell when I came back into the house to wash my hands, there was Caroline large as life in the kitchen.

'Jack, sorry, the door was open, I let myself in' she said, 'Is Julia around 'cause I just needed a word, um, a word about, um, the event at Eastnor.'

'Uh, hello Caro, no.' I said. 'She's gone to her mother's,'

'Well, her car is here,' she said.

And I thought how easy it was to lie, and how hard it was at one and the same time, how the words just fell out. I felt sick to my stomach. I needed to wash my hands. I was sweaty, and hot.

'Well, her mother came, and they went off in her car somewhere, don't ask me where.'

More lies. It wasn't easy but it all fitted together somehow. I washed my hands at the sink, and Caroline said,

'OK, well, thanks.'

She hesitated then.

'Jack, y'know, um, well, no, it doesn't matter.'

I thought then, should I tell her. Should I tell my wife's best friend, this lovely best friend who's tried to help me – us - so much over the years, that her best friend, my wife, was upstairs dead in the bedroom, and that it was me that did it, but I couldn't remember, but that she was a whore and a bitch from hell and deserved it, even though I couldn't remember if it was me or not. But if it was, then so be it and I did not care that she was dead. I said,

'No, go on Caroline, it's okay, go on, tell me, what is it?'

She said,

'Well, I know things aren't great with you two, and you know that I don't exactly approve of what she's been doing. We've been friends well, for it seems forever, but y'know, well, she's gone a bit too far I think. I've tried to talk to her, but it's no good, she won't get help. Do you know what I'm saying, Jack?'

I did, and I said,

'Thanks, Caro. But y' know, things are as they are.' Bloody stupid thick as shit thing to say. She said,

'Jack, y'know, well, you do deserve better, you know.'

She looked at me as if she might say more. But she didn't. I looked at her. She was a fine looking woman. Forty –eight. She must have been same age as Julia but she looked, and acted far better. She was straight as a die was Caroline. She kept herself fit, and firm. Not a stick insect like Julia. More meat on her. She had a great body. I'd not really noticed 'till then. What the hell was going on that I noticed Caroline now? What sort of sick person was I to have killed my wife, and then to notice her best friend in that way? But I had stirrings, feelings. Christ alive I needed help. I felt the lid was being prised right off the box that was me, my private stuff, and the stuff was going to leak out, or explode. I continued,

'I'm not sure when she'll be back, something her mother seemed to need her for. Is it urgent, this Eastnor thing?'

'Oh, no, just for a few days, a show. But it's not 'till next weekend. We were going to take the van and the horses, and set up there, y'know, retail stuff. But Jack, are you alright? You seem a bit distracted.'

Bugger. Of all the things. She would spot it, of course. I replied,

'No, I'm fine, just stuff in the garden (if only she knew what stuff) and the workshop, you know, I've got a few bits to do.'

It's funny how when you work from home, everyone thinks they can drop in and chat, that you've nothing else to do, as if you're at home relaxing. She said.

'Oh, of course, sorry, you're working. I'm really sorry. I'll call Julia later.'

And she went to leave and it was at that moment that I realised the whole time the list, the bloody list, with the body stuff and everything, had been sitting there on the side in the kitchen, where I'd left it on my way to the bedroom. Shit. Had she seen it? I couldn't be sure. But Christ alive Caroline was fit. She had one of those arses that you could just fuck the living daylights out of, if you'll pardon the expression. I'd noticed it before, but not really noticed it if you know what I mean. Julia would have given me hell if I even mentioned another woman, let alone her best friend. Caroline gave no sign of having seen the body list. None at all. She offered me her cheek, I kissed it, smelling a faint hint of perfume, and a slight body sweat smell. The lid was off alright. How could I be feeling like this with Julia dead upstairs? I was sick. Surely? I watched her drive off, then grabbed the list, shoved it in my back pocket and ran upstairs.

Right. To business. It's harder to take a dead person's clothes off than you might imagine. Bloody hard. They don't co-operate at all. Still, I managed it, bra and all. There she was, naked. Thin. Thin nose, thin face. Everything about her was thin - she hadn't always been so thin. Small bulge at the stomach, parting the hip-bones. And bloody hell a ring through her belly button. I'd have to take that out. Christ, I thought, I'd read about people who had other bits pierced too. Well, I wasn't going to look there. No breasts to speak of. Stick insect. Bird skeleton. She'd always wanted bigger breasts. Wanted me to pay for enhancements which I said I absolutely would not. She went into a rage then, full spittle and all. Christ I had to take off her jewellery too. She never wore a wedding ring, but she had two others that she said she'd bought off QVC, diamondique, moissanite or summat like that, like diamonds but not. Anyway, massive great things. And earrings. Pierced. Christ it made me feel sick touching her, dragging the rings off her thin, bird claw fingers, and taking the earrings out of pierced ears. I'd have to deal with the jewellery at some point. Right now, I stuffed it all in the jewellery box that she kept on the dresser. So, there she was, naked. Dead. And I couldn't help myself, God knows I felt sick to think about it, but it's what happened. She had always said I wasn't a real man, could I get it up or what? And there, with her naked and dead in front of me, I had the most stonking hard on I'd ever had. I touched myself, thinking, bitch, bitch, bitch. She would see who's a man or not and have my come all over her face. I thought of Caroline, her warm, wet arse, her pussy, her mouth on me, Julia had never done that. I was sure Caroline would. Caroline, with her mouth on me. Mouth on me. So that's how it was. I came all over her coldness. My warm cum, my, warm wetness on her cold flesh face. Take that you bitch!

Christ, I was sick. Sick and perverted. I sank to the floor and sobbed. Sobbed my heart out. I don't know what time it was when I got my senses back, but it was dark, and I was there with my trousers down and Julia naked and dead on the bed. I pulled up my trousers, grabbed her clothes, ran downstairs and put them in the washing, put the machine on and ran back upstairs. The carpet was heavy. Even so, I managed to lay it out, pick up Julia, lay her on it, then rolled it up around her. I heaved it up over my shoulder and hefted it downstairs, through the kitchen back door and out to the compost heap. I'd put some steps next to it so I could get some height to drop her into the pit I'd created. I mounted the steps, carpet and Julia over my shoulder – bloody hell it was heavy – and dropped her in. Then I took the shovel and covered her up, took the steps and put them away, and went inside. I was shaking. Shaking from what I had done, and from the physical exertion. I poured myself a large whisky and downed it in one. I should have gone to the police of course. I should have. Too fucking late for that now. The body was dealt with. I went upstairs again and stripped the bed in her room, stripped off my clothes and put these with the bedclothes, took out the other washing and put another load on. I hung her clothes on the airer to dry, and went straight to the shower turned it on full and let it run, and run, and run, with my head under the full blast of the water. I looked down at my body, my chest, my stomach still quite taught, my hips still quite slim, my pubes with their grey hairs showing, and my dick. So, I could do it after all. The numbness I'd had for all these years had gone. There was nothing really wrong with me, nothing wrong with my body after all.

6. Caroline

Caroline knew there was something not right with Jack when she left him at the house, he seemed agitated and not like his usual self at all, so she texted Julia.

jules is all ok can we talk?

Julia didn't reply but that was ok, she usually didn't wire herself into the mobile, and if she had gone out with her mother then anything was possible. She'd noticed that Jack had been sweaty and dirty from the garden, and wondered, was it too awful to have a secret passion for your best friend's husband? She thought think the answer was 'yes', but it had not started like that, though, more like a kind of gradual thing. He'd kind of grown on her, grown more attractive, and she couldn't tell you at all why, whilst at the same time she and Julia had grown apart bit by bit. Caroline did more listening than telling these days and didn't tell Julia the sort of stuff that she used to. She'd done a counselling diploma, and masters, and had been in counselling herself. During one of her sessions she'd told her counsellor about Jack, saying that she believed she had it in perspective, and under control. Caroline could not help herself feeling that Julia was way off though as she seemed to abuse her marriage and God alone knows what else went on. One night in the pub, for example, Pete had showed

Caroline his arm where Julia'd punched him and he said that wasn't the only place he had a bruise but he wasn't going to get his kit off in public. Even so he was smitten with Julia, Caroline could see that, while at the same time Julia made Jack out to be some kind of inept imbecile. 'Thick as shit.' she used to say. Jack seemed kind, attentive, a bit distant maybe, making her wonder if he drank but Julia had said no, and laughed saying if only he would show a bit of life in that way, be that adventurous. She would say how frustrated she was, how he couldn't get it up as much as she wanted, as much as she needed. Caroline thought Julia's 'extra maritals' were kind of accepted by them both, a sort of compromise that they could both live with. After all, there was no one perfect model relationship no matter what was pedalled in magazines and on day time TV. Caroline knew that all relationships were different, but felt that there was no point to being married if there was no union on some kind of level. She gave herself a hard time, though, asking herself what right she had to listen to other people's problems as, after all, what the hell did she know? She'd never been married but once she came close, and it nearly broke her, as if her heart was made of glass she had, like that Blondie song, and later when she was learning about the loss cycle, she believed she had been depressed over losing something that she had never had, but had come so close to. She'd never had a real relationship after that, and never had marriage but she felt the lack of it, the absence or loss of it, maybe. Anyway, she reckoned that had been at the heart of her depression, but she had never let on to other people, not Julia, not work, not her family – who never saw much as they were miles away – not anyone. She wanted a proper relationship, not one where your partner wants you to fit into the corners of his life when he wasn't busy somewhere else. She wanted a relationship where each puts the other at the centre of their world and all else revolves around it, and she thought of Jack, it always came back to Jack. It occurred to Caroline that maybe Julia didn't really want a normal relationship, and given her past, she perhaps didn't even know what a normal relationship was. Julia was maybe after abuse, sort of hooked on it, like a drug, as she seemed to seek out abuse, and almost revel in being used by men, then she would use them (or abuse them) right back. When they got serious, wanted commitment, or what she regarded as soppy, Julia would drop them. Like Pete, for example and even though he lasted longer than the others he went too in the end – only then he came back. She'd said he wanted her to leave Jack and live with him. She told Caroline that Pete had got her pregnant but she'd got rid of it. Caroline was gobsmacked when Julia told her, but Julia just laughed and said after that she'd got her tubes cut so no bastard bloke was ever going to get her up the duff, that she was her own woman.

At school, Julia and Caroline had been close, through O levels and afterwards Caroline had gone to the Tech College and done a pre-nursing course while Julia had done a secretarial course, then temped for a bit to get money to leave home and set herself up. She had always loved horses, said they were better than people, and that you could trust horses. When Julia's dad died she had a bit of money left to her, and she bought a small stable, and set up the business selling horse stuff, saddles, tack, and the like, going round shows and things. She said that her dear bastard father never did her any good alive, but dead his money was dead useful, and laughed at her own joke. Caroline helped her out sometimes when she wasn't on shift at the General, where she went on to work in A&E. They both loved the outdoors, the smell of it all, and they both liked horses, but Caroline preferred people. And talking of people, Caroline had seen Bob's car parked in Dianne's driveway more than once. She wondered what that was all about, and she wondered what was up with Jack, because he was definitely not his usual self. He'd talked to Caroline quite a bit lately, about counselling, what it involved, and what kinds of things she talked to people about. He was a real sceptic, saying it was bloody useless all that talking about stuff when people should get on with it themselves and what good did talking do? He was a real cave man, not in the big club ugh ugh sense, but in the Men

Are From Mars, Women Are From Venus sense. Whenever there was a problem, he retreated into his cave to think things over which made Caroline think about his garden and workshop probably being his cave equivalents, which was no small wonder being married to Julia. Caroline thought she would have gone to Mars itself if she'd been married to Julia, and instantly felt guilty about what sort of friend she was, having thoughts like that, but the problem was that as she became more and more distant from Julia emotionally, the more Julia seemed to rely on her emotionally. Caroline realised over time that her friendship with Julia was really all about Jack and her feeling of wanting to protect him, as if she were some kind of guardian, maybe, a real life flesh and blood guardian angel. It was, she thought, a good job he didn't pick up on any of this, or at least if he did, he didn't show it. Caroline felt tied to Julia, whether she liked it or not, thinking how she'd created her own dependency, that she and Julia went back such a long way and had such shared history, and that Julia hadn't always been such a bitch, she'd just got things all twisted up. She told Caroline once that her dad had abused her when she was a kid. Sexually. Started off touching and that, and more, said he'd teach her, get her ready for men, if Caroline knew what she meant. After the words "Bastard ruined my childhood", she didn't say much more, but Caroline could imagine the rest. The night-time visits, Julia's father's one hand held over her mouth as he got her 'ready for men', fucked her, his own thirteen year old daughter. She said she'd been terrified to go to bed, or tell anyone, relaying it all in a matter of fact sort of way, as if she was telling it about someone else to someone else. It was awful. No one should have to go through anything like that, and no wonder she left school, and home, when she did. Julia had said she'd never told her mother, and that was why she didn't go to his funeral which her mother didn't understand. Afterwards, Caroline went with Julia and watched as Julia, jaw set and an emotionless expression on her face, spat on his grave. Caroline had never seen her like that before, and then Julia simply stood, muttering to herself, over and over,

'Bloody, fucking bastard. Bastard. Bastard. Bastard.'

Caroline had to pull her away, and later suggested Julia might think about getting some help, counselling or something but Julia replied that it was no use talking about it, that it was a long time ago and that she was glad he was dead, and burying was too good for him, so was dying of a heart attack, the bastard should have been fucking cut into little pieces and if she'd had a bit more about her that's exactly what she would have done. What happened though, she went on to say, was now dead and buried. It was over, but it didn't sound like it to Caroline. She thought Julia was trying to make herself believe it was, but it wasn't. She had contained it, shoved it down deep but it was alive and eating away at her from the inside out, like a parasite. And if she lived with that inside her it would eat her clean alive, or would blow, like a volcano.

For the first time ever, Caroline had argued with Julia over Pete, and Jack, how Caroline was treating them, and who knows who else. They'd not had many words, but words enough, ending with Julia not wanting to talk about it, and storming off, saying that Caroline could sodding well sod off and leave her alone if that's what she thought, and what was it to her anyway it was her fucking life. Afterwards, Caroline had come round to Julia's to try to talk about it, she felt they had too much history to just fall out like this, and Julia had no other friends really, not real friends. Instead, she found Jack there, alone in the house so patching things up with Julia would have to wait. And Caroline had her own containment, not so parasitic, but also set to blow unless she did something.

7. *Julia Goes on Holiday*

Birds, crows. I'd swallowed a crow and it was struggling in my throat, choking me. Its beak had pierced my throat, great gashes had opened up in the front of my neck, my skin torn open, my skin, my blood poured out and out in great fountain spurts, blood everywhere. I woke up with a start, hand to my throat, gasping for breath, I was wet, covered in blood that was sweat. Not blood but sweat. Christ alive. Blue, the whole room was green, no, blue, sky, dead, what had happened to my eyes, my eyes, was I blinded? Why was it all blue? The alarm went off, and I realised I was in my bedroom with the curtains closed. I never closed them usually. The sun was shining through the blue material. Bloody hell dreams are weird shit stuff. What was going on in my brain that I'd dreamt that? I went to the bathroom, half expecting to spit or sick up broken black feathers and bits of beak into the basin, but no. I looked the same as usual. Same grizzled forty seven year old face. I leaned one hand against the wall and took a piss, hard to do first thing with a semi-erection. I pissed without paper, pissed in the bowl, a bit on the seat, and a bit on the mat. Fuck it. Splashed cold water on my face. I wondered if what had happened, had happened. I padded naked across the hall to her bedroom. There was the stripped bed just as I'd left it. So, it had.

From outside, I could hear a crow calling, I thought it must have been that bugger that infected my dream. I hated crows.

I took a shower. Had a shave. Left the shavings in the basin. Got dressed. In the kitchen I made coffee, fried up a plate of bacon and egg. I was starving. I was also shaking a bit, or trembling is more like it. A sort of inner tremble that comes from the core somewhere, not like being physically cold - that comes from outside in. This was a deep thing, an inside out thing. Like feeling sick before exams, or sick before getting married, or before Mum's funeral. I hoped it would go away. I half wanted to go and dig Julia up, to check that she was, in fact, there, and was, in fact, dead. But I didn't. I took a swig of coffee, looked out onto the compost heap, and thought about what next. I had to plan out what next, plan out the holiday, send Julia to Turkey. I made another list, and remembered I had to make sure to destroy that other list. The list went like this:

- Clothes to clothes bank
- Bottle bank
- Food shopping
- Holiday places in Turkey
- Mo
- Caroline

•Others - Bob, Dianne, Susie?

It was still early, so I went upstairs and fetched down one of the large suitcases. I filled it up with Julia's clothes. Not that I knew what I should put in there, just stuffed a random selection of all sorts. Not winter stuff though. I had to make it look realistic. Turkey – would be warm, I thought, this time of year. Was it? I went for middle ground and shoved a cardigan in and a jumper. As I was putting the things in the case, I noticed her handbag on the side, and her mobile. Shit. Mobile. I picked it up. There were two messages on it. I read them. One was from 'B', saying he needed to talk. Some bloke she was shagging no doubt. The other one was from Caroline, wondering what was up. Shit. She must've noticed something from yesterday. I wondered if I should reply to them both. It would seem odd otherwise. I'd have to think about it. Christ it was complicated. I'd need to do better than this. I fetched toiletries, and other stuff – Christ alone knows what women pack – and shut the case. The stuff I'd taken off Julia had dried overnight. I put it and a load of her other clothes in a bin sack, then put it, and the suitcase in the boot of the car. As I closed the boot a car came up the drive and scared the shit out of me.

'Hey, Jack mate, Jack are you up y' lazy bugger? Just passing.'

Bob. Bloody hell not again. He'd got the window wound down, elbow out, and said

'Got coffee on the go? Any danger of a cup, I could do with one. Hard night.'

He winked, got out of the car, walked with me into the kitchen, fetched a mug and poured himself a cup. I've never understood how Bob could drink or eat and still keep talking, but he did it. If I did that I'd choke. He was drinking his coffee, and said,

'Just, um, was just passing like, and wondered about that blow out, are y'up for it later on this week then? I'm at a bit of a loose end, like. How about Saturday night? Will she let you, waddaya reckon? Is she in, still in bed?'

I wasn't doing anything but was stuck for an answer, I didn't know if it was yes or no. I said

'Yeah, sure, why not. She won't care, you know that. Yes, um, she's not up yet (lie). Well she will probably gimmee a hard time (another lie), but that's tough, given what she gets up to I don't bloody care. What d' you have in mind?'

And all the time I was thinking about the bags in the boot of my car, burning their red hot guilty way through the car carpet and metal floor to drop on the yard, and Bob would see that Julia had not packed and gone away at all but was there dead and buried in the compost. There was the evidence, there was the case with her clothes in the boot of my car. I had to get rid of it. List item one. The case and the clothes in the case was another matter. They'd need to be buried somewhere deep, and where they wouldn't be disturbed, or thrown in the river. I'd need to weight them. Or burn them. Yes, burn them. I couldn't take the chance of them being found or turning up by accident.

Bob suggested The Anchor for Saturday, which I agreed to. Fine, anything, just let me get to the business of the clothes. And please no more visitors. Bob went off happy. Whistling. I guessed he'd got laid last night. He had probably wanted me to ask him about it, and I hadn't asked him, and I felt a bit bad about that, but it could wait. Bob's getting laid stories always lasted a long time and I didn't have the time. I never minded if he called by when I was in the garden, or the workshop because I could get on and he would chatter away and it wouldn't matter. I couldn't shut myself down, it was an effort to keep looking normal let alone speaking normal. I had to get a grip. I had to separate out what had happened and deal with it. Boundaries. I needed to get what had happened into a box of its own in my head. Then close the lid. If I could. I wondered if that made me a cold, unfeeling, bastard. Well, it might, but I hadn't done it yet. I wrote on the list,

•Ask self question, am I a cold bastard

The case with the one lot of clothes went on the bonfire pile at the bottom of the garden. I lit the (fortunately) tinder dry sticks then watched my guilt burn itself to destruction, poking it from time to time. You can't be by a fire without poking it or interfering with it in some way, it's a kind of law about fires. The dry weather was a god send, as was Dianne being away. No one to see, no one to complain, not much smoke to speak of. Nothing to speak of. I wondered if I should say a few words, as it sort of felt like a cremation. I made a mental note not to dig the compost heap for a good long while. Those were words enough. On to the recycling point. I'd tackle the mobile phone stuff when I got back.

And bloody hell who should be at the recycling but Caroline. I didn't hold with swearing as a rule but the situation called for it - fucking bad luck or what? I'd just put the bag, noting that the whole bag had to go in, not loose clothes, when she says,
'Jack, hello. What you doing here?'
So, what was I to say?
'Ah, Caro, just giving my dead wife's, your best friend's, clothes away to charity – is that ok with you? I killed her by the way, yesterday, in the bedroom. Didn't mean it, at least I don't know if I meant it or not.'
I said,
'Hi, Caro, fancy meeting you here! We were just having a clear out, or Julia was, I got the job of carting it here (lie). I've done the bottles as well. Right clued up environmentally we are, nothing wasted, paper, plastic, y'know and all the kitchen stuff goes on the compost.'

Christ, I thought, why did I have to mention that? I'd have to be more careful. Strange, though how the lies seemed to be more easy. Maybe it's like wine. I'd seen some stuff about how when wine tasting, you have to not rely on the first taste, but have another one, let the taste kind of settle. Richard and Judy, was that it? I was quite getting into wine, even though Bob laughed at me for drinking wine instead of beer. He used to joke that I was not a real man. Big tough guy like me, a wine drinker. I didn't see what was wrong with it myself. What was the rule that said I should do x or y just because that's what most people with no qualifications much to speak of, and brought up on a farm are supposed to do? Where's the sodding rule, eh? I thought about Julia saying all the time how I was thick as shit. Ok so I hadn't left school with much, but who had the money? And I'd built it up from nothing. Sheer graft, that's what and no bugger was going to take it off me. Not her, not the chancellor of the bloody exchequer, no one. Sodding government would have us living like communists. We'd nothing when I was a kid. Nothing. Farm near as dammit went under had I not taken it on for a while and sorted it. Julia knew bugger all about wine, business, money, or anything else for that matter. Except horses. I said to Caroline, 'Well, um, I'd better get on.'

She said,

'Hang on a min, Jack. Um, do you think we could meet for a drink, for a chat? I've got one or two things that, um, I wanted your advice on.'

It just seemed easier to say yes, so I said yes. I didn't want to stand there much longer with Julia's clothes so close in the recycling, even though I knew they couldn't exactly jump out and accuse me. I said,

'Yes, sure, when?'

She replied, a bit awkwardly, as if she hadn't expected me to agree,

'How about later today? Not in The Anchor, how about the Blue Boy, say, around seven?'

So that's what we agreed. I didn't think she had suspected anything. After all, what was there to suspect? Dammit. The mobile. I got back in the car and steamed home. The mobile. I'd have to ditch it. I thought, though, that it could be useful. I could, maybe, send messages, make a kind of distraction. I could say about the Turkey thing. It might be complicated. In the house, I stared long and hard at the message from Julia. What would Julia say back? Would she text? I hadn't a clue about texting. I rarely used my mobile. She would say something acid. Something about me that wasn't good. I pressed the return message key, and pressed the small keys with a bit of difficulty as my fingers were a lot bigger than the keys,

All fine j same as usual mum wants me go turkey no time explain talk when get back jules

I put Jules as that's what Caroline had called her. Would that do, I wondered? Well, I could check it out later, couldn't I? I pressed 'send'. In for a penny. I made some coffee and decided I had to call Caroline. I couldn't face her with the thing face to face. I'd have to ask her to look after the horses. Christ the horses. Shit. I thought the horses could wait. They'd be ok for today. I'd call her up, explain that Julia's Mum needed her to go to Turkey because her friend had let her down at the last minute. That she'd not had time to do much except pack and run, that she'd asked me to sort the horses, but that I wondered could Caroline do it? They were just in the next field, it was just water and feed, and the mucking out. Not too much. The show thing that Caroline wanted to see Julia about, that might come up, but Caroline might have to cancel that.

Should she go for two weeks or just one? Two weeks in Turkey. I knew bugger all about Turkey. And where in Turkey? Caroline was bound to ask. Shit. I took my coffee and got on the internet. I wasn't great at it, but I knew you could search in Google, or yahoo. I looked in Google. I typed in 'turkey holiday' and masses of sites came up, thousands. Christ alive, how was I going to work it out? Where would they go? Julia had mentioned Turkey a few times, and it occurred to me she must have got some magazines from travel agents. I searched around the living room, and bingo, there were holiday brochures. She'd even circled a few places – Marmaris seemed to be a favourite. Where the hell was that? I put in Marmaris into the Google search. More thousands of sites. I selected one, and bingo. Pictures and all. Seemed like a great place. The Russian Riviera. Looked fantastic. Blue Lagoon Hotel, now that looked great also. Spa, three pools, bars, restaurant, the lot. I hadn't realised just what a country Turkey was. Never was much good at geography. I thought it was all desert, but it wasn't. Green. Mountains, skiing, beaches, and the sea. Also, a lot of history, Ephesus, and stuff. And they produce a lot of cotton clothes, and leather, and gold. OK. I thought that two weeks was better. It would also give me some space to think. Not that Julia and her Mum would be doing any culture. Shopping – yes. Bazaars – yes. Clothes – yes. Culture – no. Julia wouldn't know culture if it got up and bit her on the backside. Actually, I didn't know much about it but I was finding a bit out. Funny what having a bit of money does, makes you want, no, makes you appreciate better things somehow. Like the whisky, like the wine. I did like nice things. I know Bob thought it odd, and maybe it was odd. I felt a bit out of place sometimes, in the pub when they were all going on about football and beer and stuff, and I'd be quiet, and they'd make fun of me for being quiet. I felt sometimes, that I sort of didn't fit. Didn't feel like one of the crowd. That's why I didn't go out much. Felt better being at home. But home was Julia, and she made me feel as though I didn't fit there either. Not anymore.

I was due to meet Caroline at seven o'clock. I had lunch, and slept for a few hours in the afternoon. No weird bird type dreams. No dreams at all. When I woke it was past five. I showered quickly, and changed. I still had Julia's mobile. No more messages. What about 'B'? I wondered about him and Pete. I added Pete to the list. I could ask Caroline, she'd know. I thought I'd sort out Julia's mother once I had sorted Caroline. I took a deep breath and rang Caroline. She answered almost immediately. I said,

'Caroline, Jack. Look, something's come up. Julia's mother has got her to go to Turkey with her, on holiday. Yes, that's right, Mo's friend pulled out last minute as she'd had a health scare or something, I don't know the details but that's how it is. Anyway, long and short is - Julia's gone with her to Turkey. It's all very last minute. She passed me a few things to sort. Horses one of them. Could you do the horses?'

I rattled it off fast so she'd have no time to think, and so that she'd focus on the horses. She replied,

'What? Where in Turkey? Bloody hell, it's a bit sudden isn't it? We were supposed to do this show! Can travel agents do that?'

Christ. Can they? I hadn't a clue. I said,

'Yes, apparently they can, y'know what technology is amazing isn't it these days.'

She said,

'Well, good for Mo. Not sure about Julia, I know they didn't see eye to eye always. I think Julia blamed Mo for the stuff with her Dad, you know.'

I knew. I said,

'So, um, see you later then?'

And she said,

'Yes, um, fine. Hang on, how long's she gone for?'

'Two weeks. Talk about it later, OK? Bye.'

I couldn't hold it together for longer. I put the phone down. Relief was not the word for it. I felt like shitting my pants. All my insides turned over. I felt weak, and sick. What in Christ's name. I took another shower and felt better. I poured myself a large whisky even though I was driving. Actually, no. I'd walk to the Blue Boy. It wasn't that far. Half an hour? If I could convince Caroline, I could convince Mo, couldn't I? Mind, I'd not done the face to face thing. Sending Julia away on holiday was harder than I thought. I looked at my list. I struck out a few things. It looked like this:

- ~~Clothes to clothes bank.~~
- ~~Bottle bank.~~
- Food shopping
- ~~Holiday places in Turkey~~
- Mo
- Caroline
- Others - Bob, Dianna, Susie? AND Pete.
- Ask self question, am I a cold bastard

I looked over the list, and added two more things that occurred to me.

- Mobile phone
- Mail and stuff

Food shopping I could do in the morning. Waitrose. I heard that thing how they were giving away paper bags that would recycle themselves or biodegrade or whatever and how they were fetching hundreds on e-bay. What a load of bollocks was that? I had a strange Julia-like feeling about the green-sandalled-muesli-belt-brigade. I thought that things would be much easier if Julia would hurry up and tell everyone that she had had a wonderful holiday, and had decided to stay in Turkey, with the Turkish army and navy. Selfish bitch that she was. But I'd have to wait two weeks. I had to get to work as well, there were some bookshelves needed making and the Hall stuff to install. And just who the fuck was 'B'?

8. More about Julia Going on Holiday

So I met Caroline in the Blue Boy. And how it came that I woke next morning with her in bed with me, I don't know. It just sort of happened. I walked into the pub, and she was already there. She said,

'Hello'.

That's all she said then and I felt something unlock inside. Something very deep, like the shaking thing, only different. Is that bad? Probably. But that's how it was, a sort of unlocking. We got to talking then about how come Julia had gone away with her mother, and her mother, and all that. I felt bad about lying but there was no other way. And we had a drink, then another. She was drinking red wine, me as well. That was good. We bought a bottle. We drank that. She as well. She said, sorry but she'd got a taxi as she needed a drink it had been a hard week. If only she knew. I said,

'That's fine coz I walked, we can share a cab back.'

That was about the most sensible thing I remember saying. She talked quite a bit about how she was sorry to have asked to see me, but she couldn't stay quiet, how she knew I was married and that but that she had to say how things were for her. And of course by the way she would do the horses no problem and it was a bit odd Julia going off like that with her mother. I stayed quiet for quite a bit of the time, let her talk, same way as I did with Bob. She went on then that this was really not a great thing to be doing, and I mustn't worry because if I said for her to fuck off then that would be fine. So I couldn't work out what she was getting at and was a bit amazed that she used the 'f' word. Thick as shit? I said,

'Caro, what is it you are getting at exactly?'

She said,

'Don't you know?'

I thought, there we are again with that woman thing about second guessing, and me thinking Caro was, maybe, after all like all those other women who made you do that. Then she said,

'Look, Jack, I don't want you to have to guess.'

Amazing! She continued,

'I have feelings for you, y'know. Feelings. Christ sake Jack. I think I am in love with you. Love you. Have done for years.'

I was stunned, and thought a whole number of stunned things in a micro second, like, well, bloody hell, Chrissake, fuck me, what about that. I said,

'Blimey Caro.'

We were sitting opposite each other in the pub, in one of those booth type things that they have. Don't ask me why, I can't recall why, but I got up, went round, sat beside her and kissed her full on the mouth for a very long time. And felt her shoulders, and waist. And she kissed me back. Yes she did. Kissed me right back. Blimey. I do remember that. I'm not so good on the rest of it, actually that's not true, I do remember but it was like a dream really. Bloody fucking great dream. Better than crows by far. I said that to Caro later in bed and she looked at me puzzled like and said,

'Crows? What are you on about?'

So I told her about the dream and she said I should not worry, it was brain-housekeeping, like dusting. Doing away with stuff. She made me feel much better.

Anyway we left the pub, sort of in a daze, at least I was, with the wine and the being in love with me, and having killed her best friend and what was happening type of stuff. We'd ordered a taxi and got back to our house. It was still 'our house' even though now it was 'my house' as there was just me, or at least there would be when Julia had made her mind up to stay in Turkey and service the militia forever, with her legs wide open, forever.

There were no words really for what it was like with Caro that first time. But there had to be words. It was loving. For the first time, real loving. I can't say what that was like really, a feeling, a sort of whole body feeling thing exploding through my cock. I loved her too. Not just in love, but real love. I knew that. I told her so as well. I said,

'You haven't asked me if I love you back.'

She said,

'Don't be daft, I know you do. I think I've known for a while.'

And I said,

'Not good enough, Caro. You deserve me to tell you. You need to make me tell you that I love you – and am in love with you. Which I do, and am.'

And we kissed then in the porch. The taxi disappeared and we were in the dark. I opened the front door and we went in, still touching, still sort of kissing not wanting to let each other go. She'd been in the house so many times. She said,

'Wait, is it alright?'

I replied,

'Of course, we're alone aren't we?'

She said then that she wondered about it, would we regret doing anything, after all I was married and Christ she was Julia's best friend and what must I think of her as a friend. She thought it was all crap, it was all crap and she should go home. She was sorry. She hated Julia for what she was doing, she couldn't help how she felt, she loved me, but that didn't justify her sleeping with me. What was done could not be undone. We had to think about it. She corrected herself, saying,

'You know, it's not sleeping with you, and it's not fucking. It would be making love with you, and there's a big difference.'

So I told her then. I told her that I thought I had loved her for a long time, since the boundary thing, since even before that maybe, certainly since before she bowled the six in the pub clear across my boundaries and unlocked me. I couldn't go back, didn't want to. I didn't want to put her in a part of my head to be let out sometimes or not. I wanted her, body and soul and spirit. I said how she was not like women I was used to – not that I was used to that many. How she, she...... I stopped then because she kissed me full on the mouth. And I kissed her back. We went upstairs, holding hands, fingertips touching, to my room. I gently pushed her down against the bed and she pushed me, gently, right back. And that's how it was. Each taking the clothes off the other, she giving me back what I gave – well, not entirely because she didn't have the equipment, but she unbuttoned my shirt and kissed my chest, pushed against my shoulders. I pulled off her clothes, and kissed her soft, soft, skin. I felt so very weak but so very strong all at the same time, feeling the blood pulsating in my crotch. Then I couldn't help it. She had her hand on me, guiding me and pressing me against her. We were mouth to mouth, kissing, exploring. Then, for some reason, we stopped and looked at each other. I swear her eyes were shining, happy. I guess mine were too. She smiled. I smiled. She laughed a bit. We both laughed.

We kissed again, this time more slowly. We lay side-by-side then, naked, and looked at each other. I'd never done that before, with the light on and everything. She was so lovely, all curve and breast. She said I was perfect, just perfect. Hair in all the right places. I knew I wasn't that hairy, but I was compared with her smoothness. She had the most smooth skin, and soft, and I smelled that same slight body sweat perfume smell that I'd smelled before. I traced her curves with my hand and pulled her to me. She pulled me to her. We carried on then where we'd left off, in a kind of slow rush to the climax. I felt like I'd come home. Caroline. I felt like crying. I was exhausted. I could smell her hair, taste the sweat on her shoulders. I pressed my face into her hair and breathed in. There was no going back from something like this. She was right, it wasn't just sex. It was far more. Where were the boundaries then? Where were mine? Fucking nowhere that's where. Everything up in the air and nothing come down, or caught, or in its proper place. All just tossed up. And what goes up.....

So she was there lying next to me, her head on my shoulder, and it was fairly early in the morning. And it sounds corny but I did think it was like having an angel in the bed next to me. Not so much what an angel might look like, but what they bring. Peace. Safety. Security. She was so quiet, breathing slowly, with such perfect features. She was beautiful, peaceful. She had this way of making me feel at ease. Julia was always so noisy. In the years we shared a bed she tossed, and turned, and snored. She was never at ease. Caroline was at ease, a forty-eight year old calm beauty. Soft shoulder length hair, with a slight wave to it, not dyed by the look of it. Fair but not dyed. Some slight grey tinges. Well, she and I were much the same age. I realised that I knew not much about her, really, not the real her. She had fine lines about her face, relaxed then as she was asleep, and not obvious. When awake her face was always lit up, happy. She had green-blue-grey eyes, not blue exactly but not grey or green either, somewhere in between, they changed like the sea and sky. I'd noticed that lately. It occurred to me that I'd noticed her quite a bit lately. I didn't think that I'd ever seen her cross or angry, or such stuff. Not even when she was pissed off with Julia. Her face never went ugly like Julia's did. I stroked her hair. This was a rare moment. Making love last night had been amazing. That's what love was then. Would it be the same if – when – we did it again? What if she knew what I'd done? Would she love me then? She murmured something, turned into me, still asleep, and put a leg across one of my legs. I needed a piss but I didn't want to let her go, or have the moment end. Wanting a piss is not something you can put off, though. I untangled myself and went to the bathroom. I tried to be quiet. Not easy. Anyway, she was awake but not quite with it when I got back into bed. It was just after seven. She asked me the time, her eyes not open. She opened her eyes suddenly and sat bolt upright.

'Shit! I've got to be on shift at eight. Christ, Jack, sorry but I'm going to have to get going. Can you call me a taxi, please, please can you?'

She looked at me. My face must have said a lot. She kissed me, and hugged me, said sorry but she really did have to go but could she come over later? Of course, I said of course. She hugged me again, then jumped out of bed straight into the bathroom, I took her a clean towel, she showered, then jumped straight into her clothes. Meantime I'd gone downstairs, made tea and toast. She grabbed a piece of toast and slurped at the tea. She was even gorgeous eating toast and slurping tea. I said so. She laughed and said if she'd known how bloody gorgeous I was in the sack, she'd have told me how she felt long ago. How many years had we wasted? When the taxi came, it was hard to say goodbye, to let go of her. I'd just found her for Chrissake. Like finding a gold seam once turning around and then not being able to find the way back to it. Was there a map for any of this kind of stuff, or a guide? Where is it all written down, and why does it all have to be made up as you go along? I was worried, not rational I knew, but I was worried that she'd have second thoughts, that I'd not see her again. That she'd think this was a big mistake and not come back to me. Or that I would discover this wasn't real. What did she see in me?

What? Would she come back? She kissed me, hard, and looked at me, took my face in her two hands. She said, as if she knew what I was thinking,

'I'll see you when I come off shift, promise, I'll come straight over. OK? And we'll talk. It's all been a bit sudden hasn't it? If you need me, call me, you've got my number. See you later.'

Then she was gone. Talk later would be good. She would know what direction, she would have the map. She was a counsellor after all. Just my sodding luck to find the woman of my life, and to know it would come crashing down if I wasn't careful. What woman would love a bloke who had killed her friend? And then lied about it, to her and everyone else. Would she love a murderer and a liar? I didn't think so. And I hadn't really told her, or anyone else for that matter, anything more about Julia going on holiday.

9. Mo, Bob, and Dianne

So I was in the kitchen making coffee after Caro had left, and the phone rang. It was Mo. Shit. She wanted Julia. I never really liked Mo. Actually, I detested her. It was more than the mother-in-law thing. She and I had never got on, not from the word go. At first I hadn't minded but over time everything about her got to me. Her voice mostly. That really got to me, a sort of very nasal, posh, Black Country. And she always ordered me about as if I was kind of beneath her, with single words not properly strung together, like 'Jack – chair', or 'Jack – door', or 'Jack – whisky. No ice'. I called her Lady Muck. Bob thought it brilliant. He said I was always good at the nicknames, like at school the Head had dandruff and we called him 'Flakey', and the biology teacher who was six foot six we called 'Stretch'. Julia hated me calling her mother Lady Muck. So Lady Muck it was whenever I could. There she was, on the phone, she said in her single words,

'Jack. Mo. Jules there?'

I had to tell her. This was the moment. If I didn't tell her now, I maybe wouldn't be able to later. In at the deep end. But I wasn't really ready, hadn't worked out what to say. I was still in a daze from Caroline and the smell of her was still on me. I hadn't showered. I was convinced that Mo would smell the sex of another woman down the phone. Stupid of course. Julia. I'd sort of put her out of my head for a bit, now she was back. Christ. All these thoughts in a few split seconds, then Mo again,

'Jack? You there? Hello?'

I couldn't put it off. I tried to remember what I'd said to Caroline, I said,

'Mo, um, sorry but Julia isn't here. She, um, she's gone off for a few days with Caroline, I'm not sure where. She just said she'd been invited to go at the last minute cos Caroline's other friend dropped out at the last minute. Somewhere abroad I think, Turkey I think she said, some resort there. I don't know too much about it, sorry.'

I was trying hard to not give too much away, to keep it vague so she wouldn't expect too much detail from me. Mo was not happy.

'Turkey? Resort? But we've got shopping! She never said! Why didn't she call? Well, typical! Always thinking of herself!' she exclaimed.

I said,

'Well, um, I'm sorry, I think she did mean to call you, she didn't have much time, it was all very last minute. In fact she did ask me if I'd let you know at some point, because she might not have time, and I was going to do that just hadn't got round to it. And you know she and I don't really speak much. Sorry Mo, I didn't know you'd arranged to go shopping.'

Lies and some not lies. It still wasn't easy, and I could almost hear Mo's brain cells whirring round, checking for consistency with her built in son-in-law lie detector. She loved to catch people out did Mo. She'd always be correcting things, like

'Well, you might think that, but in actual fact it's such and such'.

'In actual fact' that was one of hers, and the other thing she said all the bloody time was 'on that score'. All the bloody time, after each sentence almost, and sometimes twice in one sentence, like when she came over to collect some curtains Julia had got for her,

'Ah yes Jules, on that score, you know, no one else in actual fact does curtains like this. You have to get them done privately, it does cost a lot more, on that score, to get that service.'

I used to sit sometimes and just count the number of 'on that scores', and if two sayings came up in one sentence that was a winner. She also sounded the 'g' of every word that ended in 'g' as if it had a 'u' after it. Back to the main thing, though, would Mo believe me? What if she didn't? I heard her sigh, and she said,

'Well, most inconsiderate. How long gone for?'

Those bloody "g"s again, I thought, and replied,

'Two weeks, well, that's from a few days ago.'

'I s'pose nothing to be done, then. She can call me when she gets back. G'bye Jack.'

With that she put the phone down. Yeah, I thought, goodbye Lady Muck. It had been harder, and easier than I thought. The next bit would be more difficult, though, the not coming back. Would her Ladyship accept that I wonder? I'd bought myself some time. I swigged the coffee and looked out onto the compost heap. Julia would be lying there, slowly disintegrating. I wondered how long that would take. I supposed an age, but if there was organic matter, maybe less long than if you bury someone normally. Like when you bury a pet, like I did with our cat once. I accidentally dug it up because I'd forgotten where I'd buried it. It was still sort of there, a bit maggoty but a lot more had gone than I'd thought would have gone. I'd have to find out. I'd also have to sort out what to say them all when Julia decided not to come home. I pulled out the list from my back pocket, and added that to the list. The list looked like this:

- ~~Clothes to clothes bank.~~

- ~~Bottle bank~~

- Food shopping

- ~~Holiday places in Turkey~~

- Mo

- Caroline

- Others - Bob, Dianne, Susie? AND Pete.

- Ask self question, am I a cold bastard

- Mobile phone

- Mail and stuff

•Compost – decomposition

•Julia coming home – prepare for ALL

I thought maybe I needed a new list, but this would do for now. I wondered about number eight. Was I a cold bastard? I'd put Julia in a compartment in my head. I didn't regret it. Well, only regretted it from the point of view of Caroline. Bugger. Could I contain it, keep it secret? It all seemed to be working up to now, but we hadn't got to the hard part. Her not coming back. That would be more difficult. I thought that it maybe wouldn't go down as easily as explaining a short-term absence. Lady Muck and Caroline were bound not to accept it easily. They'd want to talk to her, expect her to talk to them. Would they expect me to go after her? Maybe. Maybe that might help, if I went out there. I had her mobile, she would text from there. But they'd expect her to call if she had the phone. No, the phone would have to go. One last text to that 'B' character. He had to be made to realise it was all over, whatever it was. Maybe she could go off to somewhere more remote than Turkey, like white slavery? No, Mo would be straight onto the British Embassy. Anyway, that would take thinking about.

I was in the workshop then, as I realised I'd not sorted out the shelving and cabinet for Overbury Hall. I'd added Overbury to the list. I'd rung her up, Fiona Langley-Barrett, wife of The

Honourable Piers Langley-Barrett – she'd been puzzled when I first spoke to her, that I didn't know the Langley-Barretts – and she said she'd be most pleased to have me fit the shelving and deliver the cabinet that morning. I'd packed it all into the car, and was about to set off when Bob appeared, too late to help as usual, saying.

'Hiya! Not interruptin' am I, eh?'

'Hi Bob,' I replied,

'No, but I'm just off to Overbury, y'know them shelves.'

'Ah, yes, fine, I'll catch you later then, just noticed that Dianne's back then?' he said.

'Oh aye?'

Shit, that would mean she'd have seen Caro leave in the taxi, never mind. He looked a bit as though he wanted to talk a bit, like that other time when I was sure he wanted to tell me all about his latest legover. He said,

'Ok, no worries. I'll uh, pop next door maybe, see how she's doin'. Mebbe a job or two to do. See ya.'

I said, 'Fine, ok, yep, see ya.'

He went off then, and I tanked over to Overbury to Fiona-call-me-Fi-everyone-does Langley Barrett.

On the way in the car, I wondered about Bob. What was he wanting with Dianne exactly – a few jobs? He'd always been one to comment on her size, but I knew Susie had been a big woman, and he liked big women. Was there anything there, I wondered? He told me about most of his conquests, but nothing about Dianne. He had been around a lot lately, mind, she'd been away. Just passing, he'd say, mind he did come this way a bit. I guess if had something to say, he'd say it, that was his business. After all, what was it to me? They were both adults, both single now. They could do what they liked. Susie wasn't about to create a fuss as she and Bob had been divorced for ages. She'd got a new partner, so no problem there. And as for Dianne, well her husband had long gone – he was violent so she said, and jealous, but wasn't around much so far as I knew. Anyhow, that wasn't for me to be bothered about.

At Overbury the shelves fitted perfectly. I knew they would. I'd been super careful about the measurements. The lovely Fi loved the colour of the stain, and loved the cabinet. It matched perfectly one she already had, and although you could see they were not an exact pair, it was close enough. She also wanted a new coffee table. A very large one for the very large second sitting room. Could I do that? Yes I could. Easily, and cheaply, but it would cost her a lot. She was one of those women, I suspected, who always got her way, with her husband, and everyone else. But she sort of did it nicely, in a sort of way that made you think it was your idea to help her in the first place. Not bossy and demanding like Lady Muck. This was a real lady. Out of my league, out of my class you might say, a real lady. And they had money, real money that went back hundreds of years. Not new money like mine. Old money. You could smell it in the house, a sort of old dog brass polish good red wine churchy sort of smell. All the smells of hundreds of years of living. Some people called it breeding. What the hell, anyway, she was a decent enough woman. I liked to think she fancied me, in a sort of 'wouldn't mind a roll in the sack experience a bit of the other side of life' sort of way. In that way, I sort of fancied her a bit. Wouldn't ever have done anything mind, she was a good customer, paid well. In the hallway before I left I pulled out the list to write down the job, said I'd let her know roughly how much, but it wouldn't be cheap as it was an irregular size and that. Christ I pulled out THE list. I shoved it back in my trouser pocket. I was trying to get on with the normal stuff, and the Julia thing had come crashing clean in.

I said goodbye to the lovely Fi, and drove back home, stopping off for milk, bread, bacon, orange juice and various other bits from the village Co-op. I couldn't face Waitrose. Just when I got in, Bob arrived. Christ, the bloody place was like Paddington sodding station. When would I get some peace? Well, fair dos to him, he did say sorry, but was Julia around? Christ. OK, here goes. I said,

'Well, no she's gone off with her mother (I nearly said Caroline) to some place or other, Turkey, I think. Why?' He replied,

'No reason, really, just she'd mentioned she might want some help with a horse show at the weekend, though I could give a hand as I'll not be doing much else.'

Well that's a stunner, Bob helping Julia! I said as much. He said, 'Well, y'know how it is, can't always be at each other's throats eh? Anyway. Um. Got those sash clamps in the car if you wannem?'

I did, and offered him to stay for some snap. I was starving. It was good to talk to Bob, even though half of what I was telling him was all lies about Julia and Turkey. He laughed saying she'd be shagging half the Turkish army no doubt, her and Mo both. Actually the whole army, Julia one half, Mo the other. And bloody hell he felt sorry for the blokes there. No offence Jack. Bob seemed to take it all pretty well, as if Julia going away at the last minute with her mother wasn't at all unusual or anything.

'Bloody weird some women,' he said in a distracted sort of way. 'They do just get what they want then dump you don't they?'

I thought, well yes they do, but sometimes we dump them. Really dump them. But he wouldn't know that, and I couldn't tell him. I asked him if Dianne had needed anything, and he said not much, that there was a drain needed sorting and some of the roof tiles needed replacing. Not much. He went on to the footie scores then and how Chelsea were up for it, and bloody bunch of prima donnas they were sometimes and what about that Alan Ball then only sixty-one and we weren't far off that mate and we only live once so let's make the most of it, eh? And how bloody good would it be to be in Barbados right now eh? And who did I think would win? Aussies were his favourite and he had a bet on they'd better bloody well win. I thought that he didn't really need me at all. He could hold a one bloke conversation could Bob, and even with all the talking he'd eaten all his lunch.

Afterwards he went off, and I got out in the garden. I thought sod the workshop. It was a fantastic sunny day, with a cool-ish breeze. We'd not had much rain for a bit either. I rotivated the top section ready to put in potatoes. Soil was as dry as anything and easy to work, not like when it was wet as hell, and heavy. As I worked I got sweaty, and more sweaty. I had my shirt off. Felt the sun on my back. It was good to do something physical. I didn't think of Julia, or the compost heap, or her body decomposing quietly there. I didn't think of her mother, or Bob, or scuba bloody Pete, or Susie, or Dianne, or 'B' - who I needed to text, or the phone that I'd have to get rid of, and the jewellery. Bury it. I would bury all that somewhere very safe. I thought of Caroline, last night, and would she come back. She would. Of course she would. She had to.

Dianne shouted over the fence at me could she have a word. I needed a break so I went over, and she said could she come round to the house. Well, why not, I thought, the whole world and his wife have come over or rang me up, so why not Dianne as well. So she came over, and by the time she arrived I'd had a quick wash and changed my trousers and got on a clean shirt. I grabbed a beer, and made her some tea. She chatted about Cyprus, and how really lovely it had been and how relaxing, and the boys really enjoyed it, and how would I let her know if I saw her ex-husband around because he was being a bit awkward at the mo. I thought she was looking really good, she had a bit of colour and looked as though she'd lost a bit of weight. She asked how Julia was. I said,

'Oh, well, y'know, the same only she's away with her mother – Turkey. Last minute thing.'

Dianne nodded, and said,

'Uh, hu. Yeah, well that'll give you a break then as well. How are things between you two?' She sipped her tea and looked directly at me. Strange how women can get right to the heart of it, so you find yourself right there and talking about stuff you'd never talk about with blokes. Bob had never asked me that sort of thing. Blokes just don't. You say stuff if you want to. I thought about me and Julia, how were things between us? Well just great, actually Di, because she'd dead and mouldering away in the compost, I killed her actually, and I am now free, in love with, love, and am shagging her best friend. I said,

'Well, you know, as ever. Not great. Could be worse.'

'I don't believe you Jack,' she said in return.

Christ – what had I given away? Nothing actually, because she went on,

'Things couldn't be worse. I know how she treats you. You should get divorced. Why don't you just throw her out? She's poison, a menace, you know that. Why Caroline puts up with her, I don't know. After all, you live practically separate lives anyway.'

There wasn't much I could say to that, except agree. I said,

'Di, thanks, you're right, I know that. I just can't see a way out really that won't cost me a packet. As it is, well we rub along ok, y'know. She does her thing, I do mine.'

Di was in the mood for an argument, obviously. She went on,

'I know you think that, but your life, everyone's lives could be better if she was out of here and away where she couldn't spread her poison.'

She stopped suddenly. As if she'd gone too far, said too much. I wondered what she meant then, I asked her,

'Whadday mean, spread poison? What poison?'

She drank up her tea and said,

'Well, y'know the usual stuff, look not to worry, just, well you know that whatever you decide I'll support you. Just decide to get a divorce. Take the hit. You'll be happier in the long run. You only live once, Jack. No second go.'

And with that, she left, leaving me a bottle of wine she'd brought back from Cyprus. I'd heard that before, that expression, the same. Bob had used it. He'd been round there, of course. Well, Julia wasn't doing any more poison spreading, that was for sure. I did wonder what she meant though. Maybe Bob would be more the wiser about it. I checked the time. Caro would be here soon. What to eat? I hadn't done any proper shopping. Dammit. I fished the old list from my back pocket, and set light to it over the sink. I looked at the other list, and crossed out Overbury. The list now looked like this:

- ~~Clothes to clothes bank~~
- ~~Bottle bank~~
- Food shopping
- ~~Holiday places in Turkey~~
- Mo
- Caroline
- ~~Others – Bob~~, Dianne, Susie? AND Pete.
- Ask self question, am I a cold bastard
- Mobile phone.

- Mail and stuff
- Compost – decomposition
- ~~Overbury~~
- Julia coming home – prepare for ALL
- Coffee table
- Jewellery

I fetched out some lasagne from the freezer, and put it to defrost in the microwave. We could have baked potatoes and a bit of salad with it, and I'd a few good bottles of red wine. Amarone, yes, we could have that. I'd got some bubbly too. We could have that. I'd got all that, and, I'd got a bit of time. I had another shower, shaved, I always shaved in the buff, and put on another clean shirt and trousers. I took Julia's mobile phone, and looked at the messages. There was the one from 'B'. I poured myself a glass of red wine, and texted a reply,

dont call or text again have gone away no signal will get new phone new number

I hoped that would do it. The good thing was that there'd been very little by way of mail. Junk stuff mostly, couple of bank statements for Julia. She had more money that she'd let on, the lying bitch. We had separate accounts, and a joint account for the bills, which only I ever put money into. She always said she didn't have money. Lying cow. She had a deposit account with almost

£40,000 in, and current account with about £3,000. It looked like she had money in other investments too from some of the junk mail. I'd have to wait and see what came in. I poured myself a glass of red wine, put the potatoes to bake in the Aga, and sat down at the computer to search for decomposition. I wondered if I could hack two weeks of making out Julia was on holiday. I'd have to. Too late for anything else. I hated lying to Caro. And Bob. And Di. Strangely, I did not hate lying to Lady Muck. I got a curious sense of satisfaction out of that. Felt sort of as if for once I had the upper hand. That power thing. I wish I could talk to Caro about it all. She'd understand. No she wouldn't, she'd hate me. Anyway, on with compost and decomposition.

10. Dianne and Bob

When Bob appeared in the doorway, Dianne rushed over and threw her arms around him and even though she'd only been away a week she had missed him terribly. So had the boys, well not like she had, but they had missed him as he'd been around such a lot lately, and had become part of the family in a short space of time. The boys had accepted him, so no worries there. Shame the holiday had been planned before it all started, but that couldn't be helped. They needed a break, and Bob couldn't come because of his work. It would have been great though, as Susie had taken his kids to Cornwall but sometimes perfect timing wasn't as perfect as it might seem. Anyhow, they were back, and there he was and after they'd got settled and she'd told him about the trip, she asked him if he'd told Jack yet. No, he hadn't. The thing was there never seemed to be a right time. Dianne was gutted, telling Bob that he needed to know, he needed to know what a poisonous woman that Julia was. She said,

'Godsakes, Bob, can't you just tell him? Tell him about her, tell him about us. He doesn't care about her after all, can't you just tell him? He won't care.'

Bob replied,

'It's not that easy telling your best friend that you shagged his wife, is it? I mean, c'mon. It wasn't as if it was once, a mistake, she basically seduced me and made me shag her on and off for bloody months on the strength of telling Jack if I didn't. It was a fucking mistake, you know that, but how can I tell Jack? He'll never speak to me again, will he? And now she's wanting all this stuff done with the horses and that, and if I don't do it she'll tell Jack. Oh fuck it's a bloody mess isn't it?'

Dianne, threw her hands up, exasperated.

'Bob, love, if you don't tell him she will just carry on. It's blackmail. You have to tell Jack, or she will, she will in the end. Get in first. You know she's now said to me that she'll tell my ex about you if you tell Jack about her, and you know what he's like. We can't let her carry on like this, Bob. The woman's a bloody sodding vicious bitch, and I told her what I thought of her not long back, cow that she is.'

She paused.

'Shall I tell him?'

'No!'

Bob was having trouble working out what was best. He said,

'I wish we could just get rid of her, y'know like they do in films. Get her bumped off. I've got a mate in the Regiment. Maybe he'd have some contacts, y'know.'

He looked at Di's face, and continued,

'Oh, love, don't worry, only wishful thinking. Well, anyhow, the bitch woman is away at the mo, in Turkistan or some such place with her mother. We've got a week or so to work out what to do for the best. And I'm seeing Jack at the weekend, maybe I could talk to him then, if it seems right, like.'

Dianne kissed him, and Bob felt a million dollars. He really had fallen for Di big time, but couldn't help thinking what a bloody mess it all was and why wasn't life a bit more simple and couldn't he get just one small break, just the once.

It was the middle of the day, but the boys were out on their bikes and it seemed like a good opportunity, so Bob and Di went upstairs and enjoyed each other, as they had been doing for a few months now, sort of in secret so that Di's ex wouldn't find out until they were ready. Julia had found out. She threatened Bob that she'd tell Jack about their carry on, unless Bob dropped Di. Julia hated Di, God alone knows why, and now she was threatening to tell Di's ex as well. Bob and Dianne had wanted to keep it all quite until they were ready, and Bob hadn't told Jack, he'd promised Di he'd not say anything till they were ready. That vicious Julia bitch didn't like to see anyone happy. She didn't even want Bob herself, she made that quite clear as one evening, round at his house she simply dumped him, saying she'd got bored of him, that he didn't do it for her any more, that she only wanted to fuck him to see what her husband's best friend was like in the sack. That's all it was to her, sex. It had not been at all what Bob wanted, what a fucking mistake. She'd been in the Anchor one night, and he'd had quite a bit to drink, and she offered him a lift home, then helped him into the house. Once inside, she'd asked him about his sex life, if he was, you know, getting it, and would he want a bit, putting one of his hands inside her blouse, and feeling him up at the same time. Bob didn't really know what he was doing, but the next he remembered was her and him in bed, she was wanting him to shag her, hard. She kept saying, 'Go on, harder you bastard, harder.'

It seemed like she wanted him to be rough, but he didn't do rough. Even so, after that she dropped by a few times, or met him in the Anchor first, or just turned up at the house. She was wild. Bloody wild. Bob had heard about women like her, nymphos. Never satisfied. She wouldn't speak to him outside that though, ignored him in the street, ignored him when he turned up at her and Jack's, and Bob realised he had got himself into something he found he couldn't get out of, and he knew he wasn't the only one because that Pete had turned up again, and people were mouthing it all over how he was giving her one. Then one night, Julia had suddenly dumped Bob, which he was hugely relieved about.

Later, quite by accident, Bob found out a lot more about this Peter bloke from a Aussie mate in the Anchor. It was one lunchtime, and Bob had just dropped in for a pint. There was a guy at the bar, and Bob sort of recognised him but couldn't place him but they got chatting, and it turned out he was staying in the area for a few months, and the Anchor was the local. He'd got to know some of the locals, certainly knew Julia, and this Pete. He'd got to know Pete a bit from recognising the accent, even though Pete's was Anglo-Aussie. Yeah, he knew quite a bit. Pete had been in Oz for a good while, north west, something to do with mining, he thought, but had come back for a bit to tie up his mother's estate 'cause she'd died. Apparently Pete was struck on this Julia woman, and there was talk she'd go live with him in Oz. This Pete was a partner in a mining business out there, diamonds, least ways that's what he said. What about that? Bob wasn't to think it was glamour and that, no it was hard graft mate, hard, and a tough sort of life, not a woman's game, mate. The Aussie bloke at the bar had done it for a while, mate, straight up. This Pete fellah and his partner out there were old friends from way back, and diving buddies, started off in the UK, then set up in business together in Oz or something. Did the barrier reef, and had been all over, Red Sea, and everything, wrecks and stuff, crewed for salvage work as well on and off. He'd done a bit of that himself, stayed on solid ground to do it nowadays, mate, better than all that wet shit. It's a young man's game that mate, more money above ground too, mate. They were planning the Galapagos, that's what he'd said, diving.

The Aussie drank up and left, and Bob pondered what he'd said, wondered what this Pete saw in Julia, skinny bitch that she was. Must be the diving thing. Bob preferred women with a lot more flesh on them. Dianne, now, she was perfect. He hated lying to Jack. Hated it. What sort of friend was he to lie like that. They went back a long way. Christ he hated himself for it. Keeping things quiet, like, was one thing. He'd promised Di to keep it all quiet 'till they were ready to face her ex. He'd caused real problems last time she had a serious partner, and broke it all up. Bob wanted to get hold of Julia, to tell her he was going to face up to it with Jack. But each time he'd gone round there, she'd been out and Jack was there. And, bloody hell what a coward he felt that he couldn't tell Jack. Liar and coward. He told Dianne that, and all that the Aussie had said, and she snuggled up to him, and hugged him, and told him he shouldn't worry, that he was not a coward that it was a tough call, and all the bitch-face Julia's fault. God, Di hated her. Maybe she would go to Australia with Pete, and that would be the end of that. Bob hated her. Maybe they should go to Jack together. Maybe they could help him get rid of her together, make her go with that Pete, maybe, to Oz. Anywhere, just out of their lives. With her gone, life would be so much better. Bob agreed it was a good idea, but they both decided to wait a bit longer, think about it, after all Julia was away for a few days longer, and they could enjoy just being together. That was their plan.

11. *Pigs, cheese, soap, and wax*

So I was looking at the computer screen, and was amazed by what came up. Pigs. Chrissake what'd pigs got to do with anything? Turned out that pigs had the same body fat ratio and hair on their body that humans have. Well bugger me. I thought about how I might use that with Bob one day. I imagined him talking about the cricket and me saying,

'Yeah, d'y'know Bob, how it is that pigs have the same ratio of body fat and hair distribution that humans have?'

And he would think I was mad, but he'd not say that, he'd say that was interesting, and ask me how I knew that then, and I'd say,

'Well, I was looking it up coz I whacked Julia, killed her, accidental like, and put her in the compost heap and wanted to know, like, when she would be fully gone.'

Right, I thought, I'd not say that then. Burial. Funny but I'd never even thought about the word. It said in the website that it comes from Anglo-Saxon, means 'to conceal'. Well, I'd certainly buried Julia. And autopsy, that was Greek, means 'seeing for oneself'. Weird. Anyhow, there were the pigs, little pictures of them at each stage of decomposition and you just had to click on the little icon things and they would show you a video clip of 1-3 days,

4-10 days and so on, up to one hundred days. A tiny piglet – piglets mind, not pigs - would be sort of akin to a human for decomposition. This one was 1.5k, it needed 40k to be like a human. It said that the piglets used had been rolled on by their mothers. Poor little buggers they did this sort of things to. I'd always thought them animal rights nutters deserved to get locked up but Christ, looking at this lot, maybe they had a point. Chrissake. And all about the sorts of insects and that, that get to the body. What was weird was that it went on about how the bacteria that's in the body, in the gut, turns on the body and eats the body away from the inside. Sort of a self destruction kind of thing. So, I wondered then, how weird it was that we all carried around in us the things that would destroy us, all the time eating away at us from the inside if we let them, and it was only our being alive that kept the body together. What weird shit. And all about how the gases that the bacteria produced made the body bloat out. Good job I didn't put her in the brook then, she'd have floated up. Then different gases get made by different kinds of insects and hairy maggots and such, carrion beetles, feeding on the body at different times, like different sittings. And the body sort of erupts. There's no more bloating then because the insects and the gases are different. I'd always wondered about Rigor Mortis. That was there too, how they could tell the time of death by if a body was stiff or not. It goes stiff, then it doesn't because of chemicals. Imagine that, if we weren't breathing in oxygen all the while, we'd all go stiff. I know someone who'd like that, or knew someone.

There was even a picture of a head, dead of course, showing how it had decomposed, lying there with its mouth wide open, wider than any normal mouth would be. Back to that woman on, what was it that programme, had Shoestring in it, Trevor Eve? I couldn't remember. Yes I could, Waking the Dead. That was it. Anyway she had all those bits of body in her garden so she could see how they rotted away, like. Looked sweet as anything she did, and all the time she had that going on. It was a film, though, not real but there were folks that did that sort of thing. What was really weird was that it was just like that man that killed his wife and sprayed her into the snow. You could never get rid of a body – pig or human – totally. There would always be bits of DNA in the ground, in whatever they were placed in long after the body itself had gone. Took a hundred years or more for that to disintegrate. Shit. That meant that no one could ever know. No one. If they did, they'd search the place and find her, or traces of her, even if I spread the compost heap over the veg patch, or the top field. Christ there was some weird stuff on the web. A Body Parts Farm in Knoxville. Had to be American. Only the bloody Yanks would think of something like that, bloody hell. And 'grave wax'. Whoever found that out? That you got yourself made into soap, from all the stuff going on in the fatty parts of your body, the chemical reaction makes soap. There'd be no soap on Julia. No fat. And cheese for Chrissake. Cheese! After about twenty days, the same chemical that makes cheese. So, when we die, we eat ourselves and turn into cheese and soap. It's just the way they put it, 'new suite of corpse organisms', as if it's like a new neighbour moves in. I was going to be fucking well cremated. None of this cheesy soap stuff. I'd add that to the list. Well Bloody Hell. I needed another drink after all that.

I switched off the computer, poured myself another glass of red wine, and thought about the state of Julia. She'd be well bloated up by now. Christ. My hands were trembling a bit. It occurred to me that I could give myself in. Bit bloody late for that. They'd think I did her in to have it off with her best friend. Christ. Anyhow, I heard Caroline drive up in her car. I thought I'd need to sort out Julia's car. But not yet. And her handbag. And her phone, but not yet. I'd have to check the phone for more messages. Do that tomorrow. Caroline. I heard the door go, and there she was, just as beautiful, no - more than. We sort of ran towards each other, and kissed long and hard, I felt like crying, dunno why. She noticed I was shaking. I said it was only from all the work in the garden and the stuff at the Hall, just tiredness. We ate the lasagne and baked potato, drank the wine, and she talked about her day, her work, how she was doing three days on shift now, and two private counselling, how it was all working out right lately, the counselling money was good, and she was thinking to take a course in psychotherapy. Then there was a pause, and we just sort of looked at each other and we both knew what we needed. We needed each other, physically. Christ it was like a drug with her, and I think me with her. Anyhow, there we were in bed, making love. And if I'd worried about that first time not being repeatable, I was wrong. So much for 'inadequate'. Afterwards, I got the champagne from downstairs, brought it back up with two glasses, and poured us a glass each. I'd never done that before, had drink in bed. Seemed right somehow. She sat up and looked at me, and said, suddenly right out of the blue,

'Jack, I've got to tell you, I know about Julia, and this Turkey thing.'

I was gobsmacked. What! How could she? What the hell? She could not possibly know. I said,

'Um, what do you mean?'

'Jack, you see Julia and I, well, we had a row, an argument, not like the little spats we'd had over the years, a real row. It was that same day, I think. Or the day before. I think that's what made her agree to Turkey with her mother. She'd never have gone otherwise. She doesn't even like her mother, and her mother doesn't really like her, apart from as a shopping companion. I pushed her too far, I think, I had a real go at her about how she was treating you, how she was behaving generally, you know. Look, Jack, that's not all.'

I couldn't believe it, Caroline and Julia had argued like that. I'd always wondered why Caroline put up with her, sort of wondered, but just assumed they'd been friends for ages, and that was that. Never questioned it really. Never thought for a minute Caroline didn't want to put up with Julia. Caroline said,

'Look, Jack, there's more. Sorry. Do you want to hear it?'

I wanted to hear it, and I didn't want to hear it. She continued

'Well, Julia's been, well, she's been, God, Jack. You must know. She's been seeing lots of blokes, you know that. And with how things were between you, I know you weren't, well, weren't, well weren't together, in the way you should be when you're married. Anyway, look, there was this one in particular, a guy called Pete.'

I said I knew him, scuba diver or something. She said,

'Yeah, that's the one. Well, ages back she met him doing the diving thing, turns out he had a mate that you met on honeymoon. Julia had got the dive club details from him, I dunno who that was, but anyway, she met up with that guy and his wife, and this Pete was there at the club, and not long after she started seeing him, you know, seeing him. And he was the one, you know, the same one she'd been seeing even before you got married. Do you remember?'

I thought Christ, that same guy? The nice one from the plane, this was his mate? I liked him. And we were only just married then. Caroline continued,

'Well, as things went on a bit, Julia was really rough on him, y'know, was sort of physical with him if you know what I mean, and I'm pretty sure he was a bit rough on her. Well, in the end it all finished and he went off to Australia and set up a business there.'

I said,

'Don't tell me, jewellery?'

'Yes, that's it,' she said, 'How did you know?'

'It's a long story - carry on.' I replied.

'So, this Pete, well his Mum died recently, so it turns out that he came back here for a bit to sort all that out, and he got back in touch with Julia, don't ask me how, or why. I think it was a kind of accident, but anyhow, now he wants her to go back with him to Australia. She's been a right bitch to him, but apparently, he wants her, told her he never stopped loving her even after all what had happened – can you believe it - that he wanted her to leave you and go with him. He's as mad as she is, I think. I'm sorry Jack, to be the one to tell you, but, well, you know he wasn't the only one, you know she's had others don't you? I'm not saying all this to make you feel better about us, about what we're doing. God, I feel guilty as sodding hell, but, well it sort of puts it in perspective doesn't it?'

I thought, well, yes it did, and no it didn't. I felt like shit again. I knew all this of course, and didn't want to know it. It had been there all these years, and I'd tried to pretend it wasn't happening. She'd been a cow to me, I knew that. Not a wife at all, or what a wife should be. I felt like shit. Caroline went on,

'Y'see, with the Pete thing, I told Julia what I thought, and she just went ballistic. I thought she might go off with Pete, but she chose to go with her mother instead. Guess she might want to think it all over or just get away for a bit. What do you think, Jack?'

I couldn't think really. I was imagining Julia and that Pete guy, and her dead body, and the cheese and wax stuff, and that head with its gaping mouth. I took a swig of champagne and refilled our glasses. I hated having to lie, but what else could I do? I wished I could just tell her, just to tell her. I said,

'Well, Caro, look, I guess I have known about her, and what she's been up to. We've had separate lives really for ages now. You know that. There's been no marriage, and, shit, Chrissakes there never was really. She's just used me and I let her, I know that. Anyhow if she wants to go off with that Pete bloke, well she fucking can, sorry 'bout the language, but that's how it is. She won't get a penny out of me. I just want us to be together, you and me. That's my future now, not her.'

I did wonder then if it could be Australia that Julia ended up in, rather than Turkey. Seemed a shame that she wouldn't get to fuck the whole of the Turkish army, or rather, half of it. I hadn't realised that this thing with the Pete guy went that far back. Christ. I wondered why all these guys only ever had a first name, all these scuba people. It was always Chris, or Dave, or such. I never got to know their last names. I didn't know much about Australia, but then I didn't know much about body decomposition. The internet is an amazing thing. I could look up about Turkey some more and Australia. You could get to know all sorts, like this bloke and woman were killed, and they found the guy that did it, because the time of death was later than they thought, because they'd been in bed with the electric blanket on, and that speeded the decomposition thing, so they knew that the killer could have done it after all because his alibi for the time didn't stack up. Amazing. Anyway. Looked like I had two countries to disappear Julia to, Turkey and Australia. I'd need to sort out this Pete guy, and Mo, of course. That'd have to go on the list. I'd have to write it more in short hand in case anyone found it, just in case. I'd do that tomorrow.

Caroline and I drank the rest of the champagne, I locked up the house, put the lights out, got back into bed, and we went to sleep in each other's arms. I woke early, and made us some tea. Before I took it up, so I wouldn't forget, I made a new list.

• Food shopping
• S and P
• Ask self question, am I a cold bastard
• Mphone
• Post
• Julia coming home – prepare for ALL
• Coffee table/Overbury Hall
• J's J
• My Will - to be cremated
• A or T, M and P

That would do. Nothing there that could catch me out. I took our tea up, and drank mine with Caroline still asleep. Didn't want to wake my sleeping angel, not yet. I thought for a long while, just lay there, thinking. What the hell had I done? Just what a fucking mess my life was. But not anymore. It would be better. Yes, it would be good from now on. I'd taken control, taken it back again after years of just moving along in a daze. I'd been in a daze really, nothing worth snapping out of it for. Well, now there was.

12. *Getting on with stuff*

When Caroline woke up properly, I made us some fresh tea as hers had gone cold, and we had tea in bed together. She wasn't working until much later, so we had a lie in bed. And what a lie in that was. I'd not really done that before, stopped in bed till late. Always up and on with the day, me. Anyhow, she said she had to get back to her place to sort stuff out, but we had all morning together. That was great. We even had a shower together and I'd not ever done that before. Shower? Together? In my dreams only. She soaped me, and me her. I felt like a teenager, only I'd never done that as a teenager. Soap. Christ. It reminded me of what I'd been looking at the day before. I was amazed that anyone got buried knowing all that. Far better to be cremated. We had breakfast and wandered about the garden. I showed her the sheds and the workshop, and the garden where I'd rotivated. She talked about plants and stuff, knew a lot about the names of the different flowers, their proper names too, not the common ones that I knew. I never would have thought she'd know about that kind of thing. I asked her about me, what she thought of me, was I, or did I appear cold, you know, kind of heartless sometimes. She laughed and said it was a bloke thing, that she thought maybe all blokes were a bit like that, could separate out their feelings and things into compartments, take them out and deal with them, then put them back in and move on to something else, like the car, or their hobby or whatever. She said so far as she knew, it was generalising obviously, but it wasn't intentional, just the way a lot of blokes were, the way their heads worked. Women, now, women mostly could let things bleed together and be talked about all at once, all together. Men and women were sort of chalk and cheese like that really. Cheese. I thought, don't mention cheese. Anyhow, she was great that morning, she seemed to know a lot about stuff like that, not the cheese death stuff, but the relationship stuff and how people worked. Well she would, really. I felt better that I wasn't a cold bastard, or that she didn't see me like that, but then she didn't know what I knew, that I meant I was – or could be – a cold bastard because I'd buried Julia in the compost and had looked up all about her body decomposing and that. Well, things just had to be got on with, they were as they were. Julia the bird woman. Now she had been a cold, unfeeling bitch. More like a bloke really the way she operated. She looked like a bird but acted like a cat. She was the hunter and the hunted rolled into one, just like now, she was eating away at herself from the inside out. Always in and out, only stayed long enough to get fed. It reminded me of what my Mum used to say, something about 'only a fool expects love from a cat', and 'wherever you go you take yourself with you'. She was full of sayings like that. Her life was all about sayings.

Bob turned up that morning, just to see if I was all right for the weekend. He said hello to Caroline and gave me a knowing look, a 'cat's away' sort of look. He hung around for a coffee. I think he was trying to figure out if we were, or weren't. I didn't care. He could know if he wanted, I wasn't about to tell him, but I wouldn't hide it if he asked me. I had nothing to hide. I was sure he would ask me next time we saw each other, which would probably be at the weekend. He asked me had I heard from Julia. Fat chance. Then he carried on about how he was right about the cricket, who his money was on, backed the right horse - bucko, how I should've had a bet on, not too late, better be off mate, see ya. And he was gone. Caro thought it really funny, how he seemed to talk and talk and not even wait on a reply but just carried on. She asked me should we keep 'us' to ourselves for now, and what did I think? I said I didn't mind, one way or the other, but I wasn't about to keep it a secret, neither was I about to broadcast it around the village. We agreed we'd be discreet, but not go out of our way to hide anything. The morning seemed to fly by. She couldn't stay for lunch, and she wasn't tempted by my offer of going with me to Waitrose. She left just before lunchtime. When she had gone I suddenly felt really empty. I couldn't really figure how things had moved so far so quickly, how she was so much in my life that when she'd gone it left a big space. That must be love, must be being in love. I missed her. But, I had to get on with stuff. I had stuff to do in the garden, and stuff to do for my keep. I'd have to make a start on that coffee table for her ladyship, the real ladyship not the mother in law one. I looked at the list. But first I had to get food stuff. I had to stock up and that meant a trip to the supermarket solo. I was well used to that. Bob teased me about going to Waitrose, said it was for them posh birds like you see on the telly, meeting up there for their coffee mornings and that. Well, they did bloody good stuff, and it was the nearest. Actually it wasn't. At least not now. They'd built a Tesco nearer but I'd got used to the drive to Waitrose and I was used to the way it was all laid out. I was just on my way in the main entrance, when I heard a voice call my name. A familiar voice. A one word command at a time sort of voice. Not shouting or anything, she didn't do shouting, she just did loud.

'Jack! Jack!'

Christ. It was Mo. Bloody hell. Something strangled me at my throat then. I had that bird-swallow thing. Christ, I was choking on a crow. I couldn't breathe. Mo. What the hell? What was she doing here? I felt suddenly really weak, as if someone had hit me at the back of the knees with a cricket bat. It was hard to stay standing. I grabbed hold of a trolley. I thought, what if Caro had been with me after all? What then? Someone up there must be looking out for me. But what was Mo doing here? It was miles out of her way, bloody miles. I managed to croak out the words, 'Weuw, um hi Mo,....you here.'

Bloody stupid thing to say, but anyway. She would not notice me being suffocated by a throat-diving crow. She never noticed anything beyond the end of her mascara, and she looked a little flushed, more colour in her face than usual, almost as if I'd caught her out. She said,

'Yes, it is a bit far to come but I'm on my way to, um, to meet an old friend, thought I stop and get a bottle, y'know.'

I did know. Sort of wondered if the friend was male or female, male probably, but I didn't want to imagine any more. I never thought about her having friends, never mind lovers, but then I never really thought about her. Mind, I had to give it to her, she was attractive for her age. She'd had Julia when she was very young, sixteen I think Julia had said, and she'd kept her figure. Like Julia she was slim, small, and well manicured, mind Julia was stick-insect thin rather than slim. Like mother, like daughter. I'd run out of things to say, really, but she seemed to want to say a bit more. Why did people always look like they wanted to say more to me, then not say any more at all? Dianne had done that, and Bob lately, and Caroline too. Was it always going to be something I didn't know, or that everyone else knew but me? I think I imagined it, maybe. She said,

'Julia. Heard at all?'

There she was again with that way of talking that left all the joining words out of sentences, the ones normal people used. I wondered if she was like that in the rest of her life, leaving the connecting bits out. Maybe that's why Julia was all screwed up. She'd got bits missing.

'No,' I replied.

That was true.

'Not a word'.

She said, 'I see. Well, no doubt you will let me know. Goodbye Jack.'

And she was away. I think I was in a state of shock really. What if Caroline had been with me? It had been all right thinking of them in separate places, in their own worlds really. It had never occurred to me that there was the remotest chance they could or would meet up. I mean, Chrissake, I'd never in all the years bumped into anyone in Waitrose that I knew. Not ever. And now, Mo. Bloody hell fire. I'd have to lie low for a bit, keep to home. Stick with home type stuff. I grabbed my usual trolley full, with a few extras so that it would go round two, and got myself home. This was going to be harder than I thought. I unpacked the shopping in a bit of a daze, and sat in the front room with a glass of whisky, in a bit of a daze. There was so much stuff to think about. It was a bloody mess, really. Even so, I had to make the best of it. Funny how trite stuff like that comes out when there's a crisis. Like at funerals, people say things like,

'Ah, he would have loved all this.'

As if he bloody would, he's dead, and he would most likely have wanted to still be alive, never mind appreciating his own funeral. The best I heard was Mum's family at her funeral. They came from near Cork. Everyone else was trying to make like they were gathered there for any reason but that someone had died, to kind of make the death a very far away thing, or to make out it wasn't happening. But Mum's family, her Cork relatives, they all came up and shook my hand and said,

'Jack, sorry for your loss.'

My loss? It was theirs too, but they said sorry to me. How about that? Right up front. I liked that. Maybe that's where I got it from, the directness. Julia could never understand it. She'd come at everything indirect always, from the side, sideways. Never straight on. She'd be all which ways round, as if the thing to be talked over were a bloody maze to be got into and out of in the most complex way. Someone – she - held the map, of course. She knew exactly the thing, what she wanted, and knew exactly which was the way out, making sure to leave me lost and confused. And it would always be my fault. I found out once, from the maze at, where was it, Hampton Court - not the one near London, the Henry the Eighth one, but the one round here - that to get out of a maze you just keep turning left. Every chance you get to turn, you take a left. That's the key. I wish I'd known what left was with Julia. I'd have got out long ago. Maybe what was happening was my 'left', my way out. I guessed I'd got a few turns to go.

On the coffee table was the magazine with the Turkey holiday stuff in. I looked at the places in there, with swimming pools and such. I thought it would be good to go to a place like that. Get some sunshine. Get away. All inclusive. That seemed good. I had money. If Julia didn't come back, I could go after her, try to convince her. Maybe that would be a good idea. Spin it out a bit longer. It might help convince Lady Muck. Christ, that was a narrow escape. I poured another whisky. When I'd got back, I found Dianne had left me half a dozen eggs. She kept chickens. She always had eggs. She had a few ducks, and sometimes she left me a duck egg or two. I thought about keeping chickens myself but I wasn't that keen on animals. Too much of a tie. Good old Di. It was funny how Bob had taken to doing odd jobs for her. I'd thought with his renovation work he'd have enough to do. And he was even helping Julia out. That was weird. Well, that wouldn't happen anymore. Maybe he was going a bit soft on women in his old age, a sort of reaction against the reaction from the divorce. I remember the time when he wouldn't have a woman near him, said they were trouble with a capital 'T'. Enemy's enemy is friend. I heard that somewhere. So that meant Bob's enemy was Julia – or had been – and her enemy was Di, which meant Di was Bob's friend. It didn't work with me and Caroline. She was enemy's friend. Susie. Enemy's friend is my enemy? Caroline'd fallen out with Julia, though, that made it work. I felt better.

I couldn't get on with stuff in the workshop after two whiskies. So, I settled for the garden again. I eyed up the compost heap and wondered if the bloating had collapsed yet. Probably not yet, but the compost would act like a bit of an accelerator. So, maybe. No, the collapse was about ten days as far as I remembered. Still a bit early. So I got on with stuff in the garden, doing a bit of weeding, cleaned out the pond filter, sprayed the block paving with anti moss stuff and patio cleaner. Doing something physical made things seem better. I couldn't help the feeling that what I was going through was not normal, yet it felt quite normal at the same time. I was getting on with stuff, the normal stuff. But at the same time there was this living with Julia, as if she wasn't dead at all. Well, she was dead, but it was as if she was still alive as well. The death stuff side by side with the life stuff. It's what the priests say, life in death, death in life, ashes to ashes. I hadn't realised the time. It was getting late, I was losing light in the garden, but I'd just kept going. I finished up and went inside. Caroline telephoned just then to see how I was. She was finishing late, so we'd meet tomorrow. She asked if I'd like to go over there, or she could come to me. I'd never been to her place, so I said I'd go to her place. It was all a bit odd then, her voice sounded far away, and everything seemed a bit fuzzy and far away. My clothes were in a heap on the floor. I needed to sleep. I was tired, so very, very tired, from getting on with stuff.

13. Saturday

I awoke feeling hung over. I wondered why. I'd not drunk that much. My head really hurt, and I felt as though I could go back to sleep, and sleep forever. But I knew I had to get up. After I'd showered and that, and peed on the wee mat with a degree of satisfaction, I made some breakfast. I felt a bit better. I knew I had to get on with things. Had things to do. I needed to focus, but focussing was not easy. Nothing seemed to really matter. Nothing seemed important. I ate breakfast in the conservatory, looking at the compost heap. I couldn't taste the eggs or the bacon. Everything tasted like sawdust. Not that I'd ever eaten sawdust, it just tasted like I imagined sawdust would. My mouth was very dry. I looked over the list. I crossed out a couple of things. It looked like this:

- ~~Food shopping~~
- S and P
- ~~Ask self question, am I a cold bastard~~
- Mphone.
- Post
- Julia coming home – prepare for ALL
- Coffee table/Overbury Hall

- J's J

- My Will - to be cremated.

- A or T, M and P

I was pleased at what Caroline had said, about me being like other blokes, that it wasn't a cold bastard thing, but a normal bloke thing. I had to get used to living with compartments, a bit like people have to get used to living in bungalows, when they've been used to going upstairs. Or people that live in those hi-rise flats, all in them little boxes all together. When you are in there, it doesn't feel at all like that, just looks like it from the outside. If only women would see that about blokes heads. The layout would be all different somehow, but still ok. I wondered about Susie and this Pete bloke. I checked Julia's mobile. No more messages. Good. I could just trash the phone, get rid of it. I could do the same with her jewellery. It seemed a bit wasteful. I wondered about recycling. I could do that with the phone – but would it be traced? She had some nice bits of jewellery. Even so, it would all have to go, but where? If Caroline knew, she could put it all in the incinerator in the hospital. But she didn't know. I decided it would be best buried. In the garden. Somewhere. Items 4 and 8 on the list would be dealt with. What about Susie and Pete? I could ring Susie. I'd need to check that out with Bob, maybe let Bob tell her. Pete was another matter. I'd no idea how to contact him.

There were no sent messages on Julia's phone, and nothing I could see other than on the phone or in her room. It was as if he didn't exist in her life. Not that she had a life now. He didn't exist in her death, in her being dead.

I wondered if there was anything in her room, letters and that. So I hunted around. It was weird, as if at any moment she might come in. All her clothes, except the ones I'd packed up and burned, were hanging in the wardrobe, or stuffed messily in the chest of drawers. It smelled funny, smelled of the absence of Julia. Her perfume, her smell, everything was here and in its place except her. Under the bed there were shoes, and bags of stuff. And a box. A large cardboard box that only just fitted under the bed. I dragged it out. Inside was all sort of stuff, cards from our wedding, bank statements, share dealing stuff, and letters. Letters? They were addressed to Julia Pritchard. Her maiden name. Others were to Julia Carver, her married name, my name. How come I'd not noticed all these letters, and in the same hand? I opened one and looked straight at the signature. Pete. There were quite a few of them. I took all the letters downstairs and started reading them, not in any particular order. The letters explained everything. She'd known him before we got married. She'd not met him through the guy on holiday, Caroline was right. She'd re-met him through that guy and the diving club. He was besotted with her, and from all accounts she with him, although I'd only his letters to go by. Strange how his handwriting was very like mine, sort of sloping to the right, curved and looped. All this going on, all without me knowing. There was one that must be about her being pregnant, although he didn't write the word as such, just him asking her to tell him if it was his, him saying he was sure it was, almost begging. I felt sick at the thought of it. All those years and him screwing her, and her screwing other blokes too. Like the one I caught her with, in the stable, her legs wide open, her moaning, and him on top pumping away. She was moaning a name, and it wasn't Pete. Guess he'd no idea about that. Then there was a letter where he wants her to go to Oz with him, asks her to please reply to his emails or texts, that the silence was killing him, that he was sorry he'd been a bit rough and it wouldn't happen again, he promised, if she'd only say yes. He'd been rough? Christ. I tried to get them in date order. This one was the last one, giving her his email and mobile number, but no contact address. There were no addresses on any of them, just dates. There were no more letters dated after this one. Maybe she did email him, or text, or it tailed off between them. The thing was, with him turning up he was likely to ask questions, be awkward. Unless she'd kicked him into touch again, and he'd gone back to Australia already. What was it, I wondered, that made him so want her? All these letters, and there must have been other stuff, emails and phone calls, or whatever too.

There was no post for me or her. Sometimes there wasn't on a Saturday. I wondered if this was a move by the Royal Mail to stop Saturday deliveries. They wouldn't say anything, just deliver less and less, until there was nothing to deliver. Then they'd announce that due to the very low volume of mail on a Saturday, it wasn't viable to deliver on a Saturday, so mail would be only Monday to Friday at bloody inconvenient times. And then Friday would be the next target and so on, until we were paying the same for a mail service that meant we collected the mail from the sorting office. Like in the States. That's customer focus for you. That's the private sector competitive edge bollocks for you, leading to improved and more cost-effective rubbish services. Bloody Yanks again. And AC Milan beat Man U. Well how about that. Bob'll be gutted. Not that I cared one way or the other, but he would. The phone rang. It was Bob. Yep it was a tragedy. Yep, later seven o'clock in the pub would be fine. He rang off. The phone rang again. Caroline. God I wanted to see her, to hold her really close. She'd known about Pete before I married Julia. That's what she tried to tell me that day years ago. But that was then. Now, she wanted to know what time we'd see each other tonight. I'd forgotten to tell her about Bob. I explained and she said,

'Not to worry, tomorrow then?'

'Yes, how about morning, go for a walk.'

'That would be great, we can talk then, okay?' She seemed to want to hang on then, to talk a bit more. It's like I heard once, that women want to use the phone to connect, to relate, that kind of thing. Blokes use it for practicalities, and when they are sorted it's goodbye. I wondered about that, so I kind of hung on with Caroline, asked her how she was, was she all right. I didn't tell her how much I missed her. She would know that. I wanted to touch her, reach out and have her beside me. I wondered if I should show her the letters. No. I couldn't tell her about the letters. If I did that, I was not sure I could keep from telling her the whole thing.

I decided to deal with the jewellery, and the letters. The letters were easy, I burned them in the living room fireplace. I checked the mobile one more time, took a long look at it. I decided it was more trouble to have than not. I took a hammer, smashed it to pieces. If anyone tried to text or call, they'd just have to ring the house if they wanted her, that was, if they had the number. She probably never gave out her home number so there'd be no chance of me picking up the 'phone. I mixed up a bit of plaster, and stuffed the jewellery and mobile phone remains in a small hole in the workshop wall, filled it up, and when it was dry dusted it off with a bit of dirt so it wouldn't look so newly done. It wasn't ideal. I knew that I'd remember what was in there, every time I went in the workshop. Somehow, that didn't seem too bad. I could live with that. Bloody mobiles. I'd got one but rarely used it. I thought about the secret, bloody twisted life Julia had led through having that, and the email. The letters must have been a bit risky to send, the man must have been desperate. I felt a bit sorry for the poor sod. Bastard though he was, and from the sound of it a rough bugger, he and Julia probably deserved each other.

So I met Bob in the pub and he chatted a bit about his kids, how they were having a really good time in Cornwall, and how Susie seemed to have a bloke she was seeing, and Dianne had gone for the weekend to her mother's so he would be doing her chimney or roof whatever next week and how was I then with Julia having buggered off and wasn't it a bit sudden like? He was drinking beer, and I had a pint even though I didn't much like beer, but now and again it was all right. I asked him if Susie knew about Julia having gone off, and he said no but he was sure she'd find out when she got back, but that Julia'd be back about the same time anyhow. He went on to the cricket then, and would I think about going with him to the West Indies, it would be great. Bob's idea of great wasn't mine, though. He went for the cheapest flights and accommodation he could get, so he'd have the maximum amount of money to spend on drink when he got there. And he couldn't blame lack of money on the divorce. I'd been on trips with him before he was divorced. Bloody nightmare. Four blokes sharing a room was not my idea of a holiday. It wasn't my idea of a holiday then, and it certainly wasn't now. Not at my age. He was set for a drink up, but I wasn't at all. Bob must have noticed I was pre-occupied. He said,

'Y'know Jack, you seem a bit as if your head is somewhere else. Can I ask, well, is it Caroline, y'know, you and her, y'know? You um, you giving her one?' and he made that 'give her one' arm movement.

Well, what could I say? I said,

'Bob, that's my business isn't it, but, well, I guess I can't really hide it, can I?'

He said,

'Bloody hell mate, I can't say I blame yer, bloody hell. She's fit mind, Jack, and no mistake. What if Julia finds out? She'll go ballistic. Maybe not, mind, given she's been playing away quite a bit herself, like, and what with everything with you two, y'know.'

I knew. Bob went quiet, then went on,

'Um, Jack, mate, um, while we're kind of on that, sort of thing, um, just so you know, well I should say something, well me and Dianne, we're sort of, well, seeing each other.'

I was half way through a swig of my pint, and choked a bit. I said, 'What? You and Di? Chrissake Bob, you said you wouldn't bang her for love nor money! I'm sorry mate but you've always given out like she's not your type at all. Bloody hell, Bob why d'you give all that out?'

'Oh, Christ, Jack, mate.....' he hesitated, he was finding it hard to get the words out. 'Jack. There's something you should know. I'm sorry mate. Christ. I don't know how to tell you. Mate, I've got to tell you. It's been driving me nuts, honest.'

I wondered what the hell he was on about, then he said,

'Julia, your Julia. It's got to do with her. It's all about her really. Well, me an' her well, I've got to tell you. We sort of ended up in bed one night – not intentional – honest! I was drunk and she gave me a lift home, and well, y'know it just sort of happened. I'm sorry mate. It shouldn't have happened. I was all confused about the divorce an' that. Thing is, she hates Di and now she's made out that if I don't drop Di and do what she wants, she'll tell you what happened, bust us up as mates. She said she'll tell Di's ex, and you know what he's like. Me an' Di, we were trying to keep it quiet, like. I wanted to tell you, honest I did, but it all got really, well, it got so that I got more and more in it, and I couldn't tell you, and she got me doing all sorts so she'd keep quiet. Christ, Jack, I'm sorry mate, I really am.'

Well for Christ's sake. Bloody bitch wife Julia and my best friend Bob. Bugger me. I heard Bob saying something to me. His voice was coming from the end of a long tunnel, shouting, echoing.

'Jack, Jack, mate, are you all right? Say summat.'

I couldn't look at him. Couldn't speak. What could I say? What did he want me to say? To say it's all right, she's banged most of the neighbourhood, you're no different, don't worry about it? I felt very, very, alone. Very. Why did everyone know stuff about my life that I didn't? I felt a fucking fool that's what. Fucking, gullible, fool. Good old Jack. Good old gullible Jack. My best mate fucked my wife, and that's ok. Don't worry about it. Water under the bridge. I didn't know what to say. I knew, though, at the same time, that she, Julia, would have done it on purpose. Just the sort of thing she would do to get at me. I was only puzzled that she hadn't taunted me with it, but if she was using Bob, then that's probably why. I said,

'Just the once?'

'Well, mate, um, no acshully, um , she came round a few times like, not many though.'

'In your house or mine?'

Bob replied, 'Mine, mate, mine, honest, not yours, not ever. Mate, I'm so, so, sorry. I never, ever, meant it to happen. I was drunk. It was only, well, you and she haven't been, well, y'know, not together like that for years, and well, Christ it just happened. Mate, I'm sorry.'

I said,

'Drunk the first time, what about the other times?'

'Oh, Christ, she just, I dunno, she just kind of was there, she just turned up at the door, came in and just well, took her clothes off, you know, kind of as if she, well. Christ Jack, don't. It was a fucking mistake, and Christ I'm paying for it. Look, I never, ever, meant it, it wasn't like that, not love stuff, y'know. Just, well, sex, and she, well, she just wouldn't stop. Then one day she just said stuff it and she didn't want me anymore but that she wanted some things doing and if I didn't do it she'd tell you. I didn't know what to do for the best, mate, honest. I thought, well, Christ I even thought she deserved to get sorted, y'know, for good like.'

I asked him when it had happened, and he said it had been quite a while back, over a year. He said,

'Honest, mate, it was all over real fast, couple of months at most. I didn't want to, but she, Christ it seems hard to credit it, but she just, well, I dunno, she just seemed to have this thing over me, you know, after the first time she said if I didn't the next time she'd tell you, and it just went on like that. I thought it would just end, you know, and, well, it did. She dropped me. She wanted sex stuff, you know, stuff that wasn't my thing, and I wouldn't, tying up and that. Jack, mate, I'm sorry, I didn't know what to say or how to tell you, seemed like her going away sort of, well, it sort of made it possible to tell you. Di's said I should tell you. If you don't want me as a mate, I'll understand.'

He stopped and took a long swig of beer. So did I, even though my throat was strangled almost shut. That bird again, choking me. It was weird how my voice then had no ups and downs at all, came out all flat. So, Di knew as well. Bloody everyone knows about my so called private life. Did I have anything private at all? All my life seemed to be on show, or somehow lived in by everyone else. I said,

'Bob, there's no figuring Julia. Even so, to fuck you, and you to fuck her, that's, well, there aren't any words for it. I dunno how I am about it all really. Guess we'll have to see. Thing is, I don't blame you, not really. I know what she's like. Just it's sort of, well, unexpected, from my best mate y'know? I ought to punch your fucking lights out, but I can't bring myself to. Just don't feel anything at the mo, mate.'

He looked at me, and me at him. It suddenly struck me that he must be 'B'. He was the mobile message 'B'. That was one less mystery. So much for the Saturday night blow out. I finished my beer and said goodbye to him, that I'd see him around, yeah. We didn't shake hands. I walked back home. I'd had one beer, that's all. It wasn't late. I got home, got in the car and decided to drive to Caro's house. I needed her arms around me. I needed some sanity, some peace. I'd only been there once before, to collect Julia for some reason or other I couldn't remember. It kept going round in my head. Bob, my best friend fucked Julia, and I'm fucking Caroline, Julia's best friend. How does that make me any better than Bob? It doesn't, except that I fucked Caroline when I knew Julia was dead, not behind her fucking back. Even so, he thinks what I'm doing with Caroline is behind Julia's back, because he had no idea she was decomposing into cheese in the compost. So we are even then. And the Julia whore fucked the whole world's husbands, and ex husbands, and, seems like, anything male on two legs with working tackle, behind my back. That thought did not make me feel any better at all. Suddenly those ads came into my head, about the sexually transmitted diseases you could get from who you sleep with, and all the other people your partner has slept with too. Chrissakes. I wasn't about to go to any pox clinic to get checked over. Anyhow, she and I hadn't done anything like that for years. I rang Caroline's doorbell, she opened the door, I pulled her to me and held her close, breathed in the scent of her. Then I looked up and saw, standing behind her in the hallway, a bloke I'd never seen before.

14. Pete

Pete was going quietly mad. He'd been packing up his mother's life, and packing up her death, and the funeral had been bloody awful. Not much of anything and not many people, not much by way of sun, not much wind or rain, not many friends and not many relatives, and he was her only son. It was all over quickly, at the most twenty minutes in the crematorium, then to a neighbour's for not much to eat and not much drink, a not much sort of day in all respects. He'd had one eye on his mobile since he'd arrived in the UK, but the thing was that he hated being back here. He'd hoped never to come back and had tried to persuade his mother to join him out there, but no go. The business was going well, and the profits were decent, though it was hard work and things had taken a bit of a dip recently, with some talk that a recession might be on the way. He had the idea that you couldn't go wrong with diamonds, though, at least he hoped so, and life there was far better there than England and the great thing was that there, he could forget. There was nothing for him in England, only Julia being Julia and even after all this time, she was still here, and the most frustrating thing was that no matter how hard he tried, he couldn't forget, not really. To him she was like one of those imploded stars, a black hole that pulled him in, sucked him and all his energy to her. He'd never been able to properly let her go and here he was again remembering the time when, after all those years they'd met again at the dive club, and he found out she'd got married. Married! Her! He could hardly believe it. He laughed when she told him, God, how he laughed, and she laughed too and she teased him, kept waving her wedding ring in front of his face. It didn't stop things though as the first chance they had, they were kissing furiously, and couldn't wait to get at each other. She still wanted him but got a kind of weird sexual pleasure from him not fully having her. He said she should get divorced, go with him and get divorced, but she wouldn't, she would only say that he wasn't good for her, that she couldn't rely on him, said she never said she didn't love him, on the other hand, she never said she did. Pete wondered if he knew what love was, or if she knew, and he felt like there was a piece of her buried deep inside him, like acid burning away unseen on the inside, and if she was the acid, then she was the alkali as well. She could fix him if only he could have her. Was that love, or a kind of love?

All those years. He thought back to when he'd first gone out to Australia, to the remote north west when there were not many folks about and geology was his thing then, in fact it still was, deep down. He loved it, but didn't get to do much these days, being more in the management of it than the doing. It was nineteen seventy six when he'd joined up with a group of geologists, and they'd gone out to the Pilbara region, then they moved on to Kimberley, and he teamed up with some others in a joint venture when he'd no money himself, but his saint of a mother loaned him some for a small stake. He spent the next seven years on and off with the team mapping out the geology of the area. They'd believed passionately that they would find diamonds as the place was so right for it because some had been discovered there in the 1890s, but the source was never pinpointed so for a few years they went down dead ends, cold trails, and were teased and led along by tantalising clues that turned up and then came to nothing. Once, they found some rocks in Smoke Creek that they thought might be it, but, no. Then, later in Ellendale some Kimberlite pipes, and bingo, but it worked out to be just too expensive to try to extract it, just didn't cost in. They were back to square one.

On an extended trip back home to raise a bit more money with a couple of the others, he'd met Julia, quite by accident. They bumped into each other literally, or she into him, more like. She had reversed into his car and that was the start of things. Love, infatuation, call it what you will. Madness at first sight maybe, madness, yes that was the right word for it. She invaded his body, his head, and his heart, and she'd kind of stayed there ever since. He went back and forth for a bit after that, tried to get her to go back with him, tried to explain to her how fantastic it all was, how she would love it, about Lake Argyll, the dam, the mountains, the rugged space but she didn't want to go, she said she wouldn't leave England. She said there was nothing there for her, and he had no money and nor did she, and she wasn't about to rough it. Then on one trip, she told him it was all over and he remembered calling her a cold-hearted bitch. She was just that. She could be hard, cold, kind of ruthless, and he'd loved that about her as in many ways she reminded him of himself, a sort of mirror image.

In the next few months they made the discovery they'd been looking for - several stones in the creek bed, that's all it was at first and he knew that they'd been there before. But, back tracking, they found more, and then they found themselves on what would prove to be one of Australia's greatest diamond pipes. It didn't seem to matter to him in some ways, but in others it made all the difference. Sometimes you find what you look for, but you don't always get what you want. There was a Stones song about that, Pete had seen them perform it live, and he'd made it his song, his and Julia's. He threw himself into the work with the team, and forgot for while about Julia but she was still there, buried deep inside him, burning away unseen. The find turned into a mine of some order which they called "Arbroath", after the place where several of the team came from. It was soon producing diamond ore by the hundreds of tons, blasted out and transported for processing by massive excavators and dumper trucks that seemed to get bigger and bigger each year. Pete didn't have much to do with the day-to-day processing part, but he'd been over there masses of times to supervise stuff, the crushing, scrubbing, and gravity-separating out, then final x-ray sorting. Arbroath diamonds were now known all over Australia and beyond for their hardness, their unusual and complex atomic structure. Sometimes, he found himself looking at the landscape, the machinery crawling all over it, and the men working. He couldn't quite believe what they'd achieved and it was all down to him and his four partners, their hard work, their bloody-minded persistence. He and the others flew regularly to Perth to check out the finished product of rich coloured champagne, rare pink, cognac, and dazzling classic white diamonds. They were sold as far away as Antwerp, Bombay and Belgium. He'd paid back his mother, eventually, with more besides, and he made sure she was ok for money, not that she ever wanted anything. It was his dad's money really, or the money she'd had from when his father died, the insurance payout. His mother had been over to visit him, and she did like it, but she didn't want to stay, as she told him - at her age she couldn't cope with the change. Pete had gone out for a while with a woman quite a bit older than himself, and she'd said something a bit the same about not wanting to change her life too much as she was happy the way things were. She would see him from time to time, and was happy to take him to bed and screw him senseless, but that was enough.

He knew from what his mother had said, some people thought he must be rich, being a partner in a diamond mine, but it didn't quite work like that. It was a business like any other, really, just the stuff they produced was different. Not that he talked about it a lot, mind, he sort of kept quiet about it because he knew what people might think if he said what he did. That is, only in England. It didn't matter back home, because people there knew what it meant. If people asked usually he just said he was a miner, or a geologist. Things like that, big things, were just normal there, everything was on a different scale. He thought he had a good life all things considered, he had a decent house with quite a bit of land with not a bad income and money to do what he wanted, to come and go and it not to worry him. He'd had offers from girls, almost married one, had taken up a few invitations of the physical kind, but he had never settled. He had developed a real taste for older women, they were undemanding, grateful for the attention, and knew what to do with a man's body. He'd met someone in England a while back, and to spite Julia he'd had a pretty wild affair with the woman in a way that he wanted, which was undemanding, no strings, glorious, uncomplicated, sex. He hadn't intended to, but thought he might give her a call, give her one last good time. He reckoned he'd not be back again now, not unless it was for business. Time to burn his bridges, so he'd call her up and now that his Mum had died, this would be the final tie with England cut. One last fuck.

On one of his previous trips back to England a while ago, he visited a dive buddy from years back. Steve, the mate, and he had done the Barrier Reef together and they'd stayed in touch. They were at Steve's dive club one evening, when who should walk in, but Julia. Turns out Steve had met her on the plane on her honeymoon of all things. Pete's heart was thumping.

'Just like those bloody diamonds,' he thought. 'Nothing for years, then there's this trail that leads right to the pipe.' Married or not, he believed she was his. He felt she belonged to him. Deep down she was his, and his only, and he was going to get her back. Crap thing was, though, that he just couldn't get her to see it. She seemed to want him, but she would not commit. She just kept saying they weren't good for each other. What sort of crap was that?

This time, he'd rung Julia from the airport, as soon as he arrived. He'd MSN'd her but she was totally rubbish at returning calls and texts. So far they'd met up four times and each time was more frustrating so they'd argued, big time with her the same as ever, lively and exciting, but infuriating as hell. She was teasing him, he thought as she always teased him, to his face and about how she'd been with other men, but he didn't care. She had punched and kicked him sometimes, but he didn't care. She liked it a bit rough. She was wild, a wild woman but he loved it, and they'd argued like a long time ago, and she'd said he'd never tame her, said he was her keeper, and she was his wild thing. He'd said he didn't want to tame her, that he wanted her wild, but she wouldn't stop seeing other men. That made him mad as hell. She said no one told her what to do. He wanted her to want only him. But she wouldn't. When they argued it was hell, but it was like a ritual – first hell, then heaven. They argued, fought, and she gave in then, gave in to him. He couldn't believe it when he'd seen her that time at the dive club, she was still fabulous, with her thick blonde hair and blue eyes, and her slim almost skinny figure. Then, he'd felt that small piece of her buried inside, bubble up to the surface and same feeling came back this time as well, only this time it didn't bubble up, it rushed up and over like a torrent of storm water. Uncontrollable. He hadn't intended to tell her, he really hadn't but he couldn't help himself. That argument, that last hell / heaven argument, and they'd argued, yes, but that was just the run up, wasn't it? Hadn't they intended to take it further, to rough and a bit more than, for him to tame her wildness? Hadn't they always done that, when she'd been a bad girl? Why was it different just because he'd been a bad boy, a very bad boy? Had he misread something? He was confused. Was it four times he'd seen her, or five. He couldn't remember but what did it matter. He blotted out how he'd gone to see her. How it had all started like it used to, and then it was not like it used to be at all. And she wasn't, as he had thought, in the house alone. He had left her in a hurry, drove straight back to his mother's house.

The one neighbour had done quite a bit of packing up, so he was left to finish boxing and bagging up the last of his mother's things. Black sacks for the skip, bags for charity, boxes for charity, because he didn't want any of it. He wondered what would be left of his life when he went. Nothing much. No kids even. It would be as if he'd not lived here at all really and he knew that life wasn't a rehearsal. He had one shot at it and already he felt he'd wasted quite a bit as far as women were concerned, burned up some chances. What was he chasing now? And he asked himself, not really expecting an answer, what was he running from? He looked around him. Was it worth it? Was any of it worth it? What the hell was the point of any of it? The house was practically bare, as the auctioneers and the Full House people had taken most of the furniture and things. There was nothing left but a kettle, couple of cups, and some teabags. The neighbour had left a note and some milk. No fridge. He'd be on the floor tonight, unless he checked into somewhere or kipped at the airport and he hadn't thought of that. It was good that he was going back as he just wanted to get away, to leave this fucking useless bit of his life and get on with the rest. Then he suddenly had this feeling that he needed to talk, to someone, anyone. No, not anyone. The plane back left the next evening, but he needed to find someone else first, someone else. Caroline. Julia had often mentioned her best friend, and she had pointed out where she lived once or twice, and maybe Caroline could help sort things out, she might be able to help him persuade Julia, just maybe. He just about remembered where Caroline used to live, and he was sure he'd be able to find it again, and possible that she was still living there, so it was worth a shot. He didn't even think to check what time it was. He set off in his hired car for Caroline's.

15. The two of us

'Jack, um, Jack, come in,' she said, 'I wasn't expecting you, um, Jack this is, this is Pete. Pete, this is Jack. Jack Carver.'

Caroline motioned to the bloke, and I got that crow swallow choke thing again. This was Pete, the Pete Julia had been seeing on and off all those years. Chrissake. I couldn't get any words out.

So next thing I knew was we were all three of us sitting in Caroline's lounge, drinking coffee. Fuck's sake, drinking coffee. I couldn't get my head round it. Him, Pete, my wife's lover of God knows how many years, and Caroline, and me, all together in her house. Life sure played out some strange hands. Chrissake I should have gone for him, but somehow having missed the moment, the time just sort of passed by. I couldn't do that anyway, not with Caro there and it being her house and all. So we sat there, being polite, with our coffee, not saying very much. Caroline said 'Pete, well, Jack, Pete arrived about half an hour ago, Jack, wanting to know how Julia was, if I knew anything. I told him that she'd gone to Turkey, for a holiday.'

Yes, that was it, to Turkey. She wasn't mouldering away in my compost heap being eaten be beetles and fly larvae – not worms, mind, everyone thinks it's worms which would be nice but it's not, it's fly larvae and shit like that – she was in Turkey enjoying a holiday with the mother who she hated, and who hated her. So much for my peace. Caroline looked gorgeous, I just wanted everything to go away, for it to be just me and her. Now there was this Pete. I said,

'So, Pete, you, um, you here for long or what?'

He said, 'Going back tomorrow.'

He took a swig of his coffee. He went on,

'Look, I only called by to see if Caroline knew how Julia was, and it seems she's ok, so it, um, may be best that I just clear off, so…..you two, um, y'know.'

Caroline stayed very quiet. I looked at Pete, and though deep down I'd always kind of hated him, I knew that it was a kind of hating from a distance, a sort of hating without really knowing why it was I hated, like hating a food but not having tasted it. He was the unknown food stuff and I was tasting him for the first time. He wasn't that bad in the flesh. Like most things that you hate, or that scare you, if you face up to them they aren't that bad really. I kind of felt sorry for him. Poor bastard. Fancy being besotted with the bitch Julia. He was better looking than me, I thought, more rugged looking, but not as tall as me. Bit more muscle maybe, thicker set. I had more hair than him, though. He dressed well, I thought, obviously spent a few bob on the label gear he was wearing. I wondered how old he was.

'It's ok,' I said, 'Just, um, well sorry to hear about your mother, y'now, I mean I lost my Mum not long back.'

'Thanks,' he said, 'we weren't close but even so there's been a lot to do, sorting out, that kind of stuff. And the place is a bit bare now they've cleared it out. Guess I'll be off, book in somewhere, y'know.' He finished his coffee.

I knew how it was, to lose your Mum, and I remember how disconnected I felt with everything. Chrissake I found myself feeling a bit sorry for him. Poor bastard had lost his Mum, and now he'd lost Julia, although he didn't know that. And, strange though it seems, and God alone knows why I did, but somehow I found myself saying,

'Well, look, if you've nowhere, then I've got plenty of room.'

Me, saying that to the bloke that'd fucked my wife on and off for years. And Caroline said,

'Well, why don't you both stay here?'

And I said I thought I should be getting home, that my place was maybe best, that they should both come over to my place, because I had plenty of room, and it wasn't far. To be honest, I had a real yearning then to be in my own bed, with my own things around me. Having a five-bedroom house suddenly was a real asset, and better than Caroline's two-bed terrace, nice though that was. Pete said he wasn't sure. He looked at me for what seemed like ages, sort of intense like, searching my face for something, as if looking for a clue, or as if my face was a map he couldn't figure out. Then he said

'OK, if you're sure.'

I was not at all sure, but then there wasn't much I was sure of, so what did it matter? I didn't mind. He said so long as he caught the flight the next day and he did have some things to collect from his Mum's, but he could do that on the way to the airport. I hadn't realised until then just how much of an Aussie accent he had. He really had. Like he suddenly wasn't a Brit at all. Caroline just looked at me, as if, well I wasn't sure as if what. Something had obviously gone on before I'd got there. She would no doubt tell me later. At least I hoped she would. So we did that. I drove me and Caroline back to my place. Pete followed in his hired car.

Life has some weird shit in it, it really does, really. There we all were in my house - my wife's best friend, my lover and partner (was she?), my wife's on-and-off lover and soon to be ex lover although he didn't know it, and me. I needed a whisky. Caroline kissed me and went off upstairs. In the car she'd told me how Pete had turned up out of the blue, raving about Julia, how he needed to know, was she all right. She'd had to calm him down, and had told him that Julia'd gone to Turkey but she didn't tell him anymore because she wasn't sure what to say and maybe the less she said the better. She said she wasn't sure how much he knew about Julia, or if he knew Mo, so she hadn't mentioned that because he might just go asking there and that would mean trouble. Pete had seemed to calm down then, and it was not long after that, that I arrived. I poured myself a whisky and asked Pete did he want one. He did. I got ice. I love ice with whisky. And so we sat in the lounge and drank whisky together. And we talked. Or rather, he talked. He talked about life in Australia, how fantastic it was, described it as free, said it was easy to live there, mate, not hard like over here. He used the word 'free' a lot. Free, freedom, not like over here where people are always about their accent or the school they went to, or the type of job, or where they lived. None of that over there. People just accepted you. And the lifestyle. He said,

'It's bloody good, bloody hell mate y'shud see it, be there, mate, y'can do all sorts, an blimey mate y'know no one cares who y'are or where y'from. Bloody great, mate. Great. Honest. Mind, sheila's 're not much I recken, bit y'know, well not like here, mate, not like, well, y'know, I like the more mature woman anyhow if you get what I mean, but anyhow, the life's great, hard graft sometimes, but great.'

I didn't have a clue what he was on about, but half a bottle of whisky in, I didn't much care. I said

'Yeah.'

We had another drink and he said,

'Godda nice place here mate, bit like mine. Well, y'know mate, your, your Julia, sorry mate but y'know, she an' me, well, you seem like a decent guy, mate. You an' Caroline, that's a thing is it, with you two?'

I didn't answer him. He drained his glass. I refilled it, opened another bottle and refilled mine. He carried on,

'You an' Julia, you never were really, y'know, and I guess neither were we. She never wanted me, mate, not really. She stuck with things here, y'know. She didn't like what I wanted, y' know, deep down, well anyway mate, you knew about me an' her, she said you knew. Blimey, I don't blame you, mate, you could lay one on me by rights. Her mother, now, she was a right piece as well, like mother like daughter, eh?'

He went on then about his mother, how good she'd been to him all her life, her funeral and how bloody horrible it all was, and bloody hell he hated funerals, not that he'd been to many. He was slurring his words, and I saw the room was all blurry. Everything seemed to make perfect sense, in a fuzzy, tired, kind of way. I wondered if he'd met Mo, or just knew about her from Julia. Good job Caroline hadn't given away about the holiday, just in case, and good job he was going back. I was finding it hard to focus and closed my eyes. Pete seemed a decent enough bloke, I thought. I didn't say anything much, didn't know what to say. It's like they say of some people, that they make more sense when they keep their mouths shut. When in doubt, say nothing. Motto of my father. Strange how his motto came into my head then. Bastard was no good for anything, but he did have one or two sayings. Must have got that from my mother. She had sayings. I wondered if Pete's Mum had sayings. I was going to ask him, when he said,

'Y'know mate, she an' I, well, it wasn't going to happen y' know. Not likely. Tried to get her to though. Sorry, mate. Not keen on the life out there, y'know. Didn't want to rough it. Wanted rough, but didn't want that kind of rough, if you get my drift. And I did something, well, something I wasn't proud of, mate and that kind of put the lid on it. Was you she was married to, mate. Not me. Thought we'd cut up rough once too often, gone a bit far. Gave me quite a scare. Know what I mean? You awake, mate?'

I vaguely heard him. I heard my mother's voice, one of her sayings, 'Everything annoys you, and the cat breaks your heart.'

Julia, the cat, the stick-insect. It all made sense, of course, whatever it was. It was all very clear. He was sitting opposite me. I had my eyes closed and must have dozed off for a few minutes. Next I knew, Pete was flat out on the lounge floor, snoring, his whisky glass tipped sideways next to him. I looked at him then, and caught sight of myself in the mirror. God I looked rough. I couldn't focus really. Who the hell did we think we were, the two of us? We were opposites - me hating her, he loving her. We should be fighting, punching each other's lights out. I could punch him now, kick him. I wished I could hate him, this man. I didn't even know him. He was in her life all those years, but the poor bugger, he wasn't in her life at all really. How could I hate him for not being in her life? I couldn't blame him. She never let anyone in, not even him. Or she pretended to, which was worse, and then bang. Out. And who the fuck was he anyway, just some guy, some guy who fell into her. A big fat moth crushed by her. Eaten alive by her. Sucked dry and spat out. This was the shell of him, the left over, the bit she didn't want, didn't need. Maybe along the way he crushed her a bit, too. I liked to think he did. Good on him.

I suddenly realised Caroline was upstairs. I should be with her. I'd had a shit load to drink, and Chrissake, not even that much whisky could drown out the mess I was in. I looked at him on the floor. Pete. Poor bastard. I still didn't know his last name. What a fucking mess. Everything was all upside down and not in its right place. Now he knew about Caroline, but that didn't matter. What did he mean, I wondered, about cutting up rough, and when was he talking about? Who the hell did we think we were, the two of us? Just who the fuck?

I poured myself a huge glass of water, drank it down, then went upstairs and found Caroline half asleep in the dark, in my bed. She murmured that she hadn't wanted to go to sleep without me. I found a blanket and pillow, went downstairs to Pete, helped him onto the sofa, put the pillow under his head, and covered him with the blanket. So much for five bedrooms. He didn't wake up really, something about 'really good mate, mate' and carried on snoring. I went back upstairs with two glasses of water, stripped off my clothes, brushed my teeth so my breath wouldn't smell so bad, and fell into bed. I drew Caroline into me, her back to me, my arms around her. She curved herself into me, as if that was the way we had always slept, like we'd done this a hundred times before. At last, I thought, she was with me, totally and only me, and me with her. I breathed a deep and complete relief into the darkness, noticed the curtains weren't closed but I wasn't about to move one inch from where I was, and slept.

16. The Return

Sometimes time, hours and days and that, goes by really fast. And sometimes really slow. I reckoned that the world went round slower sometimes, just to be bloody minded. When you wanted it to go by fast, it seemed to hang on in there and last an eternity. So it was with the days that followed.

That morning when I woke up, Caro was fast asleep still, not in my arms as we'd both rolled about all over in the night, but there she was, still with me. I put on my dressing gown and went downstairs. I liked to walk about in the altogether, but with Pete downstairs I thought better of that. In the living room he was fast asleep. It was still early, just after seven. Worth trying to keep a bit quiet then, but the keeping quiet didn't work. He came into the kitchen, holding his head, and said.

'Blimey, mate, skinful or what?'

I passed him a glass of water, boiled up the kettle and made us some tea. Bonza. I went into the conservatory to drink my tea, and he followed. So there we were, both looking out into the garden drinking tea together. By now Julia's bloated body would have collapsed and gone all creamy. Hairy maggots. Carrion beetles. Maybe because of being in the compost, the cheesy stuff and a new suite of corpse organisms would be visiting. In her death, she would have more company than she'd had in her whole life. And my visitor knew none of this, of course, that he was looking out onto the very spot where she was decomposing away. She was in Turkey to him. He asked me why I thought she'd gone. I hadn't a clue. I told him that we'd pretty much led separate lives for years now, that what she did didn't bother me, really, it was her own business. So, I'd no idea, just that her mother had asked her. He seemed relieved at that. He asked me if I knew when she'd be back. I said I didn't know exactly, in a few days maybe. I made more tea, he asked about a shower and stuff so I sorted him a towel and said he could use the downstairs bathroom, or the main one upstairs. Mine was en-suite. Off he went, and I went back up to Caroline. She was wide awake and wanted to know I was, how Pete was.

'Fine, I'm fine,' I said. I lied because I'd had a really bad dream. 'He's ok too, maybe a bit hung over but nothing a shower won't sort out. How're you doing?'

'Oh, not bad,' she replied, 'Just, well, last night we didn't get much of a chance to talk really. I'm sorry about Pete, I'd no idea he would turn up. And you know, well, he seemed really worried about Julia.'

He'd no need to worry, she was beyond worry. But I did wonder why he should have been worried. I'd not told Caroline about what Bob had told me, what we'd talked about in the pub. I thought I'd best tell her. She was amazed.

'What? Bob and Julia? Bob? Bob and Dianne? Are you sure?'

'Yep. Well, it's not as if I'd make it up is it?' I said. 'Anyhow, that explains a lot, about why he'd been helping Julia out, and why he'd been round Dianne's place – and mine for that matter.' She couldn't get her head round Julia having knocked off Bob. She said that Julia had not said a word to her, and anyway it was strange because Bob simply wasn't her type, too podgy and not tall enough. She'd always gone for tall, rangy, rugged, kind of guys. Like Pete. Obviously like Pete. Poor bugger. Caroline went off to have a shower, and I fished the list out of my trouser pocket.

- S,M& P
- Post
- Julia coming home – prepare for ALL
- Coffee table/Overbury Hall
- My Will - to be cremated
- A or T

Not a bad list. I could delete Susie, as Bob would take care of her. I could probably delete Mo and Pete for now. I'd have to decide about her coming back. Would she come back from Turkey? Or go to Australia to be with Pete? Or, she could go straight from Turkey to be with Pete. That would solve the immediate problem with Mo, but she'd eventually want to talk to Pete, she'd find him and speak to him. I should cross out 'A'. Chrissake, could I keep up the story? It would mean more lying to Caroline. I hated that. I wanted to tell her what had happened, or tell her I didn't know what happened. That I'd done whatever, and put Julia in the compost as it was the only thing I could think to do. But Julia was her best friend, or sort of. And if I did, that would be the end of things with us. Was there an 'us'? We needed more time. I wished we had years stretching ahead of us, like most people do, with a normal job, a home and family and stuff like that. That's all I'd ever wanted really. I didn't want any of the complications I'd had to live with, the pretend marriage, the no kids, the sham couple life. I wanted kids, family, school stuff, family holidays, grandkids, retirement. I never told Bob this, but I envied him his Susie and the kids. They were divorced, ok, but it was a normal sort of divorce. Loads of people had relationships like that. At least he and Susie got on, or sort of got on, and he had the girls. He had more of a family than me. What sort of weird thing had I lived with all these years? Not normal, that's for sure. I'd only ever wanted normal. What if I told Caroline? What if I said,

'Look, Caroline, you know I said Julia had gone with Mo to Turkey, well she didn't. I made that up. I found her dead in the bedroom, in her bedroom, and I think I hit her and killed her by accident, only it may have been deliberate, only I can't remember, and I buried her in the compost heap because it was the only thing I could think to do, and I'm not sorry, and I thought that no one else would be sorry about her being dead, just that it seemed like the right thing to do, I thought it was the right thing. If I did wrong, then I'm sorry.'

It wasn't great was it? Sounded like Tony Blair's goodbye speech. I wondered if I could make up that she attacked me, or that we had a huge row, that she provoked me. What could I say to Caroline to explain how it had come to that, after all those years of Julia bitching at me, getting at me, calling me Jacky. When I thought about it, they were such small things, name calling, nothing really. But day to day they all added up, I guess. And then, me not being able to get it up. I just couldn't do it. That made her start with the little finger, waggling it at me, she knew it would make me feel crap, and angry. When she did that, I'd get out into the workshop, or the garden, do some heavy digging or machining some heavy oak planks. When I went over these things to myself, they seemed rubbish things, nothing that a person couldn't sort out, or take in their stride. Not worth killing someone for, surely.

I couldn't lie any more to Caroline. Not unless I had to. Even then that wasn't great. Can lies ever be justified? The more I lied, the worse it would get. I thought about truth and honesty, and guilt.

Can a person even justify withholding truth? I remembered something from history, somewhere they'd argued that warped kind of line, Nazis was it? Or Nixon, was it him that was economic with the truth, or that if people believed something was so, and you knew it wasn't, you just didn't correct them, even though you knew what was the truth. After all, what they didn't know…..
Caroline had once said to me about truth, that it was less about truth and more about responsibility. That was it – guilt and responsibility. She'd said adults accepted their responsibility, and there was no need to feel guilt but every adult needed to be responsible and face up to that. That was what being adult was all about, against being a child. That's what I had to face up to, that I was responsible for Julia being dead. At least I thought I was. It nagged at me that I just could not remember what happened, from finishing up in the workshop, to standing there in the bedroom with the tea. I always took Julia tea. A sort of habit. I was a lot earlier that day than normal, but even so. She was never coming back. It would be odd if people could return from the dead. I didn't believe in all that after life bullshit. And those mad blokes that made out they were in touch with the afterlife, they could make up anything they liked and who could say it wasn't true? What a load of bollocks was that? What if people could come back, like Hitler, or my dad, or Henry VIII? What then? I'd give my dad a right going over. It makes no bloody

difference when they say about the so-called spirits they are in touch with, because you get nothing out of it at all, only spirit bloody rubbish messages that are impossible to figure out and could mean any bloody thing at all. Of course they are made up. If they were real, or any good, they'd tell you real meaningful stuff, like – watch out for such and such 'cause of such and such, and they'd give you a name, or so and so is robbing you blind in this way or that, or put a bet on this one, or that. Bloody rubbish all of it. Needed their heads examined that's what. Point is that a lot of poor suckers believed them and, for Chrissake, paid them. What kind of crap was that?

If Julia returned from being dead, I wondered what she would say, but I didn't get very far with that because Caroline came back in from the shower, rubbing her hair dry, and asked had I heard about Tony Blair resigning and about bloody time, even so, it was bitter sweet. I hadn't heard, as it happened, but bloody about time was right. She put the radio on. She said she still couldn't get over Bob and Julia, and Bob and Dianne. That was far more interesting than Tony Blair. She went on then talking and asking me stuff that I'd no idea about, like what had Bob been thinking of? And, why hadn't Julia said anything? And how come she hadn't noticed anything? And what did I think of it all? That last one stopped me in my tracks. I didn't know what I thought of it at all. I got in the shower and, eyes closed, let the hot water run over my head and body. Bob and Julia. The thought of it made me feel sick. I didn't blame him though. At least he had the guts to tell me, eventually. I should 'phone him to let him know I was okay about it. He'd be worried, I knew what he was like, a real worrier about stuff. So what would Julia say if she was back from the dead? She'd probably give me hell for not having done this or that in the house, or ask why was the lawn grown up so much, the hot weather was no excuse, call me a lame-o, make some acid comment or other about something, say how she was going to leave me, useless bastard that I was, and that she was going to Australia with Pete. Would she have, I wondered? Would she have gone with him? He seemed to think not, that they'd had some kind of row or other. Maybe that's why he was all bothered round at Caroline's.

I soaped myself all over, rinsed, got out, dried, shaved, cleaned my teeth, and got dressed. The usual routine. I did not piss on the toilet seat or the carpet. Pete and Caroline were in the kitchen fixing breakfast when I got downstairs. I could smell bacon frying, and fresh coffee. I didn't mind one little bit that they were there fixing breakfast together. It had been an age since anyone made me breakfast. So we had breakfast in the conservatory, overlooking the rain soaked garden, and chatted about this and that, and then Pete said he best make tracks, had to collect his stuff from his mother's and meet a friend at the airport. Good timing, I thought. It did feel a bit odd him being there. Down to me, I knew that, because I'd invited him, but even so, it was a bit odd what with him being Julia's you-know-what. By rights we should be out there on the lawn six paces apart, pistols levelled, or slashing at each other with swords or sabres, white shirts billowing in the sweaty grunt and thrust.

Caroline had said to me once a while back that there was no such thing as a 'typical' relationship. She'd said there were some typical situations that people found themselves in, but in general there were many types of relationship, many ways of making a relationship work, and that I shouldn't think there was one to hold up as the ideal to aim for. She said I should try to make what we – that's me and Julia - had work, that I should not search for the impossible, because in not achieving it I'd maybe feel I'd failed, and that would not be a good thing. But how could I not feel I'd failed? I wasn't sure I was searching for anything really, or that I had any kind of ideal in my head. Even so I felt I'd failed. I knew what I wanted. I saw what other people had and saw that other people seemed to make things work out. I wanted a bit of that, the working out. Was it so wrong to just want to love and be loved back, to have someone want only you, and want that to be forever?

Guilt and responsibility. That was another thing. I felt no guilt at all as far as Julia was concerned. I made a note in my head to talk to Caro about that more. I'd have to add it to the list. I said, 'So, Pete, bye then.'

We shook hands on the front drive. I noticed that it wasn't just wet, it was soaking. It must have rained a real load in the night and through the early morning. Everything was hung down, the wisteria weighed heavy with it all, and was dripping. The scent of its blossom was everywhere. The sky was iron grey. He said, 'Bye then mate, I'll um, mebbe drop a line in a week or so, or mebbe you can ask her, tell her I called, and, um, just say that I'm okay with everything. I'm just gonna get on with things now. It's finished for me over here now. Okay? Thanks for everything mate, if there's anything ever……'

I thought, yes, yes, just go, bloody hell, just get on with it, go back to Australia, there won't be anything ever, and let's hope we never set eyes on each other again. I said,

'Of course, same here, Pete, bye then.'

Caroline said goodbye, and gave him a hug. So he drove off, and there we were, with a few days to ourselves, hopefully. And bugger me, just when we'd got inside, who should arrive but Bob. He didn't just walk in this time, like usual. He rang the bell, knocked and shouted. At the door he shuffled a bit from foot to foot. He said Dianne was on her way back, and he was going to meet her at her place, but he'd not slept a wink from thinking about it all, and he needed to just check that I was alright with everything and he wanted to know if we were still mates. Christ, it was like being back at school, only this wasn't about nicking pens and lunch money and stuff. I couldn't say what I thought, but I did know what happened wasn't all down to him. He'd been through a tough time with Susie, I could see all that, and how Julia would have wanted to add him to her trophy cabinet. I knew it wasn't his fault. But why should I be the one to always back down and give in, make large? Why did everyone think they could do stuff to me and everything, me, would be the same? Did they think I didn't have feelings, didn't have, or want, a life? So, I invited him in. We went back a long way, did me and Bob. Caroline gave him a hug, and said it would all be all right. She told him that Pete had stayed over, miracle or what? Could be that Julia might end up in Australia and wouldn't that be good all round. I didn't tell them what Pete had told me, that as far as he was concerned it was finished. If they thought it was all over with Pete and Julia, I'd have no chance of sending her out there, dead or not. Best keep quiet on that score. Bob again said how sorry he was, kept on about it. I told him to shut up apologising, or it would be the end of our being mates. So we laughed about it. Laughed. I'd not done much of that lately, as if I'd forgotten how to do it; it felt strange as if it didn't fit me properly, like having new teeth fitted. Then Bob said, a bit quietly,

'Y'know I'm real glad Julia went off with her mother like that, because I was a bit worried, like. She and I had had a real barney that day or the maybe the one before, and she just whacked me one, y'know, really hit me, and I hit her back like. Hadn't meant to, Jack, and I was a bit worried you know, didn't mean it, it was, well, just a sort of reaction, sort of instant, like when a bloke hits you, you just whack 'em back, don't you? And I just went off then, should have checked she was all right, but anyway…. please for god's sake don't tell Dianne, she'll think I'm a right woman beater. Anyhow, not to worry. It's all alright innit? Anyhow, best be off next door.'

And Bob went to be next door for when Dianne got back. And Caroline and me, we just looked at each other, and god alone knows why, but I sank onto the settee, put my head in my hands then, and sobbed, real shoulder jerking sobs.

The night before I'd woken in a cold sweat. I had this nightmare about sea creatures. I'd been up to my waist in a deep running stream, things like sting rays only with raised eyes on stalks on the top of them that stood out above the water, were swimming by. It was my job - god alone knows why - to help make sure they got through, to the sea I think, only that bit wasn't clear. I just had to help them get back, they had to get back somewhere, they were returning home, wherever home was. Then one of the ray things looked at me with its sticky up eyes, rose up with its wing things stretched out, and smothered me round the face. It was cold, slimy, suffocating. I couldn't breathe, and I choked up a crow, then a magpie, then a swallow, one after the other, covered in slime and bile, my throat raw from their claws and beaks scratching as I retched, and I woke up, gasping for breath. They say if you ever die in a dream, it means you are really dead. I never got that because if you never woke up how would you know about the dream in which you'd died, because you'd be dead. So how do they know? Anyway, Christ alive, I thought, Bob. Bob had done what it took me years to do, or maybe had never done after all. Had it been Bob then, and not me? When had he been round to my place? Must have been when I was in the workshop. Had it been him then? I couldn't think what to do then, or what to say, or how to explain to Caroline why I was crying. Grown man like me, crying. I couldn't tell her. I was just sobbing away, making great gulp noises and she was making shush noises back to me. She had her arms round me, comforting me. That made it worse. That made it better. Christ I'd no idea what to do, or say. I thought that if she stayed much longer I'd end up telling her the whole lot. She should go, I should be alone. But I wanted her to stay, I didn't want her to go from me, not ever again. But if I told her, she'd go, and I'd be alone, without her. It all kept going round and round in my head. Caroline, Bob. Did he kill Julia or did I? Caroline said,

'Jack, Jack, love, it's all been a bit much hasn't it, all of it. Eh?' She got up, went to the kitchen and brought back two mugs of tea. I had calmed down a bit by then, and I felt a complete bloody nance. I'd not ever cried in my whole life, so far as I could remember. Not when my dad died, but then that was good riddance. Not when Mum died. No way I was going to let anyone see me cry, leastways not Paul or his partner. She would have wanted me to be strong, anyhow. What bloody sort of a man was I, then, to cry like a baby, and in front of Caroline? What the hell was wrong with me? She asked me what she could do to help, if I wanted to talk about it. I told her about the dream. It was all clear to me then, how my life had been suffocating me, was suffocating. The ray thing was the dead Julia come back to life, the birds were maybe the lies I'd told, being fetched out into the open. Julia had returned in my head to take revenge, to kill me. Bloody hell it was worse living with her dead than alive, and bloody hell fire my head hurt like hell. The boxes were burst open, the boundaries shot to pieces. She was dead but still grinding me down. There were no boundaries anymore, and no secrets. I knew that if Caroline asked me, I would tell her anything, everything.

17. When things don't work out, and work out

Caroline left Jack's and was driving through the village on her way home, when she decided to take a detour. She knew Jack loved a particular sort of whisky, and she thought to get a bottle for him, cheer him up. The only place nearby that she was certain to get some was Waitrose. She parked and went into the supermarket, and someone caught her eye. Someone she hadn't at all expected to see. She thought it was her mind playing tricks on her. It couldn't be. It wasn't possible. Maybe it was, maybe they'd arrived back early. Just as she was puzzling it over, the someone saw her. Mo said,

'Hello Caroline, how was Turkey? Wasn't expecting you back quite so soon.'

Caroline was in total confusion. She felt sick. What the hell was she talking about? She hadn't been to Turkey. What the hell did she mean? Jack had told her Julia had gone to Turkey with Mo. But here was Mo asking her about Julia and Turkey, so Mo obviously hadn't gone with Julia. Jack had told her it was Mo she'd gone with, so why did Mo think she had gone to Turkey with Julia? It didn't make sense, unless......she couldn't think straight, but couldn't get any words out. What the hell was going on? She managed to stumble out,

'Um, Mo, well, what a surprise, you don't usually shop here, do you?'

'That's right,' Mo replied,

'I'm on my way back from seeing a friend off at the airport, and, I needed to get a few bits and pieces.' She carried on,

'So how was it?'

'What?' Caroline was still confused. Stunned by seeing her. She shouldn't be here, she should be in Turkey. Unless they'd come back early, but even so, she'd clearly not been to Turkey. None of it made sense.

'The holiday? You know, your holiday?'

'Um, yes, the holiday, oh, um, you know, Turkey, yes, great country, lovely scenery, um, great views. Well, must get on, bye.' Caroline had to get away, get out of there. Mo gave her the usual look, as if something nasty smelling had got under her nose, and walked off. Caroline managed to get the whisky, pay for it, get back in the car, and drive home. She was on auto pilot. She was amazed she'd made it home, as she didn't really concentrate on driving at all on the journey back. Her head was full of 'whats' and 'whys' and 'hows'. It was hurting her brain trying to work it all out. By the time she got home, she'd got a few possible scenarios together, or maybe not scenarios exactly, questions was more like it. This had to be about Jack. He was the key. How did Jack know Julia had gone with Mo? Did Julia tell him, and if so, why when it was clearly a lie? Pete. It could not be to go away with Pete, because Pete didn't know where she was, and was told she'd gone with Mo. Caroline couldn't figure out why Mo thought she'd gone away with Julia. Was it Jack trying to cover up something or had Julia lied to Mo and Jack? If Julia hadn't been in Turkey with Mo, and she hadn't been in Turkey with her, she wondered where the hell she had been, and, if she'd been somewhere, was she back, and what lies had Julia told Jack? Caroline felt as if she was losing her mind. None of it made sense. Pete couldn't have told Mo about her going with Julia, because he didn't know where Julia was, or at least he made out he didn't know. He seemed relieved to find out that Julia had gone with Mo. Could she trust Pete, she wondered, maybe all that was some kind of cover for something, but what? And why would he want to do that anyway? She wasn't sure if Jack had told Mo that Julia had gone with her, or if Julia had lied to both Jack and Mo. It couldn't have been Pete, or anyone – maybe Bob? She went round and round in circles. She just couldn't figure it out. Like that song, she had more questions than answers. They always played that on the waltzers at the Fair. No matter what year, no matter what generation, the songs were the same. Funny that.

Caroline had naively assumed that all was right in the world. Yes, Julia had behaved really badly to Jack, she knew that, she'd been a right bitch, in fact and Julia's going away had broken something open in Caroline, allowed her to finally tell Jack how she felt, and wonder of wonders, he had felt the same. It was amazing, and she still couldn't quite believe it, that after all the years she'd known him, this strong feeling for each other had been there, just under the surface. It didn't take that much for it all to come out, it didn't need the presence of anything or anyone, what had been needed was an absence, the absence of Julia. It was like a graze on the skin, or a hypodermic stuck in and pulled out, one sharp sting and there it all was, the bright red bubble of colour that was them, together. She had thought that they'd talk about Julia coming back, that they'd work out how to tell her about them, and when, that Jack would get divorced, and everything would be fine, eventually. It wouldn't be easy, of course, but it would work out. He would move in with her, or Julia would move out, and she'd move in with him. They'd either sell his house or hers, whichever way round it didn't matter, they would be together, he'd said that, and more - that she was his life now and that was all that mattered.

And now this, she puzzled, this about Julia, and she couldn't work out what the hell it all meant. Caroline suddenly had a thought, like a thunderbolt and she felt sick again, of course, she realised, it was Jack. This was all about Jack. It was Jack after all, at the heart of it. Typical, and she felt it all click into place and make complete sense. It could only be that Julia had deliberately disappeared, gone off with someone, and to make trouble, to get at Jack, she'd told a whole pack of lies about where she was going. Of course! Caroline felt relief flood through her like some kind of drug - not that she was into drugs, well, only when she had to give them to patients - she'd never had a general and she often wondered what it must be like to feel the anaesthetic taking over, as you fell into the deep sleep it induced. It couldn't be a normal sleep, but it was hard to know sometimes what was normal sleep. Unlike Jack she didn't dream that much, or didn't remember her dreams. She had to tell Jack. Talk to him. Not that they needed to find Julia, though, she could stay lost forever as far as Caroline was concerned, as long as she turned up to sign the divorce papers, that would be enough.

'Bloody woman', she thought, 'Some bloody friend she is.'

And then she had another thought. What if, what if Julia thought that she and Jack were an item, or suspected they were, and what if she had disappeared deliberately because of that? She needed to talk to Jack and as she'd not got to go to work for a couple of days, and she'd only got one counselling booking for the next day, she could get over to see him again, or he could come to her, no problem. No, she would go and see him, talk it over. It would all work out, it would. It had to.

While Caroline was wrestling with the 'how come Mo is not in Turkey' question, Bob and Dianne were having dinner, with Dianne's two boys. When the boys had bolted their dinner and gone off, Bob told Dianne about what he'd told Jack about him and Julia. Dianne was amazed.

'You brave boy,' she said, 'I'm so proud of you.'

Bob said that the moment was just sort of there, that the words were out of his mouth before he knew what he was saying, if she knew what he meant. She did. She kissed him on the cheek. She said Julia was a complete and total cat-bitch from hell and deserved everything she got. She went on to tell Bob that she'd had words with Julia herself not so long back, and that she'd slapped her across the face, downright bloody cheeky cow that she was. Maybe that had been the wrong thing, but she'd just lost it when Julia laughed at her. Dianne said again that she was right proud of Bob, that he had done the right thing. He said,

'Mind, I've not done the right thing, have I? Knocking off another bloke's wife, and me best friend's wife at that, I know she was a bloody yo-yo knickers, but anyhow there's no call for it, Di, I don't feel good about it at all, I shouldn't have done it, you know that, don't you, and you know I'll never do anythin' like that again, you do know that don't you?'

Dianne did, of course know that. She said telling Jack was the right thing. It was. She asked about how Jack had taken it, and Bob told her,

'Not good really, but we both slept on it, like, and I was beside m'self, so I called in earlier and that's when I saw Caroline was there, and we chatted like, about it, and I think it'll be okay. He's a decent bloke, Jack, salt of the earth. Wouldn't hurt a fly. He could have punched me, y'know, when I first told him, and I wouldn't have blamed him either, but he didn't, didn't get angry or anythin', didn't say much, just looked, well, sort of sad really.'

Bob went on to tell Dianne about Pete, and the whole thing with Caroline, and how he'd found her there at Jack's, with Jack was more like it, and how they were seeing each other, in the biblical sense, if she got his drift. She did. She asked about Pete, what he was like, and Bob told her about him so far as he knew, and while they talked they cleared the dishes, and then Bob got on with fixing some broken guttering with the two boys helping, like it was his house, and his family, and he and Di had lived there all their lives. And while up the ladder, Bob cast what he thought was an expert eye on Di's garden, from a sort of bird's eye view. Her beds were in good nick, some lovely bedding and bushes and such. Not that he knew any of their names, mind, but he would comment about stuff in the garden like he did know, annual, perennial, evergreen, that kind of thing. It had impressed Susie once. There was a cleared area up the top of the garden that he'd not noticed before. He used to have a vegetable patch, not that he'd much success what with the rabbits and insects and such eating their way through his efforts, but he was an enthusiastic gardener, and he stuck at it, laughing off the blackened carrots and caterpillar eaten cabbage. The potatoes, mind, had been a big success. He'd go out into the cool, scented evening, with his spade, and dig some up for Susie to cook and put on the table.

'See them taters,' he'd say proudly to the girls, 'See them? Your daddy grew them. And see them carrots? Your daddy grew them too.'

'Did you dig up any rabbits, daddy?' They'd asked one time, as if rabbits grew in the patch as well. They may as well, the number there had seemed to be. In the end, he'd had to put a chicken wire cage all round, but he then found a few dead with their eyes all bulgy so he reckoned they'd got the maximosis or whatever it was that did for rabbits, and good bloody riddance to them as well.

Since the bust up with Susie he'd been living in a flat. He missed his veg patch and his evening collecting. This patch Di had would make a brilliant one. It would need a bit of attention, boost up the soil a bit, and he could grow some lovely stuff in there. Might even be as good as Jack's. Jack. Now there was a thought. Jack had some great compost, real good rotted down stuff. He'd have to ask him about it, get a few barrowfuls. He would talk to Di, and then Jack. As he climbed down the ladder he felt really pleased with himself. This weekend had been awful, it had all gone pear-shaped what with Di away and then the business with Jack, but somehow from things not working out at all, it was all working out just fine.

18. Truths come home

It's strange how things come to you, when you're not thinking about them, like stuff you go to sleep with that's a problem and you wake up with the answer in your head. It's as though there's something going on even though you are not thinking. I wondered why that was, why my brain was working out all the stuff without me. And it did all that at the same time as giving me weird dreams. I wondered who my brain was working for, me or Julia. Anyhow, Caroline had gone off and I had decided to get on with some work in the workshop. I had the coffee table to sort out for the lovely Fi at Overbury Hall. Dark oak, that would do it. It was amazing how big she wanted it but I guessed big would suit her living room. Probably everything in her life was big. House, furniture, men even. I reached in the back pocket of my jeans for my measure, I usually kept it there when I was working, but I'd forgotten that I'd not been in the usual working way of things for a while, and instead I fished out a piece of paper. It was the list,

•Post

•Julia coming home – prepare for ALL

•Coffee table/Overbury Hall

•My Will - to be cremated

•A or T

•Failure - talk to C

I realised I'd not thought at all about how to handle Julia's coming back. There hadn't been anything much in the post, that was a relief. The will thing would have to wait. I still wasn't sure about A or T. That was all about Julia's return. I had to think about Julia coming home, and Australia or Turkey together. Maybe I should sleep on it. Let my brain do the work for me. It was only a couple more days. A couple more days and I could expect the calls. Mo would call for sure. Caroline would want to speak with Julia. They'd want to know why she wasn't answering her mobile. I had to talk it over with Caroline, I could maybe hold her off by saying I should be the one to tell Julia about us, that it would be too difficult for Caroline to do that herself or the two of us, that it was best I do it alone. And then I could say that Julia had freaked and didn't want to speak to Caroline. That would work. But Caroline would want to try to talk to Julia, she was that sort of person. It was not good. Julia would have to go away again. It would have to be T or A, Turkey or Australia, but which? Given the Pete thing, maybe Australia wasn't a great option, but Turkey was even less great. Caroline would believe Julia had changed her mind, she would. She would want to believe that, and she wouldn't think I would lie to her, after all, why should she? The thing was, would Mo? I could string Mo along for a bit, play dumb for a bit, see how things went. The will could wait. I thought of how Julia's body would be now. I remembered the picture on the internet of a human hand, one month after death, buried 1.2m below ground, without a coffin. Cheese flies, carcass beetles. It hadn't been a month yet, but Chrissake, the thought of it, that I'd buried her without a coffin. Well, maybe the carpet counted as a coffin. I should have felt guilty, but I didn't. I didn't feel anything. No, it couldn't wait. Instead of the workshop, I sat down at the computer and emailed my solicitor asking her to change my will so that I'd be cremated. I was sure there would be a form or something, but at least I'd started the whole thing off now. If I told Mo Julia had gone to Australia, then it would mean that Pete would be in the frame. Did I care about that? I sort of did really, Christ knows why.

I got the rotivator out of the shed, and rotivated the top part of the garden, ready for planting out. As I went along, I imagined I was peeling the skin off the earth. When I'd finished, it was red, and raw looking. It always amazed me how the soil was red, like a real living thing, and not brown like I'd seen it in other places. My great grandfather had driven agricultural vehicles, so it goes in the family. My Mum used to tell me stories of grandpa, how he'd still like to get up in the cab at eighty years of age, bloody dangerous he was too by all accounts. I'd always liked tractors and engines, and machinery and the like. I liked the thought that maybe a bit of him had come down to me, that I was carrying on the same kind of thing, close to the land, even though my closeness was about personal growing stuff and not to earn a living. Those days were long gone. There was no way I would ever go back to farming, not after what happened with Dad. Too many bad memories. It brought back the memory of my youngest brother, the dark coloured patches on his face, marks from the way he had fallen, his pale, pale, face apart from these strange shadows. I don't think my mother ever got over it.

I washed myself clean of the sweat and dirt, had a drink, and a bite to eat, and took a walk then. I found myself at the church. Strange that, because I'm not a religious person at all, just looked up and found myself right in front of it, with the great yew that they say Kilvert sat beneath, stretching out over me and across the sky. I thought to go in to the church to sit for a bit in the peace. There's a funny kind of peace in churches, and a particular sort of quiet. I wanted some of that peace, and some of that quiet. There was a notice on the door. It read, 'Closed during working hours for renovation of the bell tower'. I'd never really thought of churches as work places before, but of course the vicars must treat their place as 'work', with God as their employer, and I wondered was the praying a kind of work, and I wondered how they asked for holidays, or if they prayed when they wanted to take a sickie, or if that sort of thing happened at all in God's workplace. I was glad I had always worked for myself. It was the devil's own sodding problem tax and VAT wise, and I did have sleepless nights sometimes over it all, but at least I had only myself – and maybe my accountant - to answer to. So I sat on the Kilvert bench and took in a little peace, the peace of the churchyard. There was no one else around at all.

Across the way there was another churchyard, or at least a grassy area, consecrated and all. I had made the gates for it. I was really proud of those gates. There had been a ceremony and everything, with the ground consecrated by the Bishop. Real nice bloke he was, not at all snotty. It wasn't a churchyard at all really, but a small grassy area that would be a churchyard one day when folks got dead and were buried in there. There's big business in death. Happens all the time, and is as sure as hair needing cutting. I remember seeing a list once, of all the sorts of businesses that there were around in the town a hundred years ago, and it struck me that there was only one barber. I reckon blokes didn't cut their hair, or they mostly had someone do it at home, the wife maybe, or a maid. I supposed that someone had to work in the death business. I knew a bloke who'd made a fortune in Wales as a coffin maker. He talked about all the rivalry and that as if it was some sort of mafia, like the Sopranos, only they were Welsh and it was a different kind of death business, not making death but dealing with the after death. They had good voices, mind. He was a tenor, and he sang in the local choir before he went off to Wales. Sold him some lovely American oak once. Too grim for me all that death stuff. Yew trees are very quiet. They don't rustle, and they aren't busy waving about like other trees. I liked that, the silent stillness of the yew. If I was to be a tree, it would be a yew. This one was hundreds of years old. It must have seen a lot of births, deaths and marriages, lots of Sundays, heard lots of sermons and bells, soaked up tears. It was all very quiet now. A buzzard was up above, cruising the thermals. A couple of Sparrowhawks dropped down from the hill, and were chased off by a crow, a carrion crow. A young fox, I thought at first it was a cat, trotted out from the hedgerow and along the path bold as anything, caught sight of me then darted away out of sight. I should hate foxes as they got a Di's chickens from time to time and she went ballistic, enough so that after the third time she did get the low voltage electric fence that I'd said from the beginning that she should have. But I can't hate them, it's just their nature, they are born and raised like that. That's just the way things are. Back at the house, I saw Caroline's car. I felt something tighten in my chest, a sort of excitement. She wasn't in the car, and I wondered where she was. Maybe round the back. She'd not rung or anything, but I was really glad to think that she was here. I went round the back of the house, and found her sitting in the steamer chair on the patio. She got up and put her arms around me. I held her tightly, close to me, almost lifted her off the ground, and said,

'It's great to see you, Caro, I wasn't expecting you, you could have rung, let me know. I might have been out somewhere.' And she said,

'Jack, it's great to see you too, and I thought to come over, you know, spur of the moment, just needed to talk to you about a couple of things.'

We went in the back way in to the house, through the conservatory and into the kitchen. She had a carrier bag with her, with what looked like a bottle in it, wine maybe. I hoped she would be staying, I thought that I must ask her to stay over. I put the kettle on. She said,

'Jack, look I need to talk to you.'

I looked at her, and could see a kind of frown on her. She looked a bit worried. Suddenly I was worried. I didn't want to ask, but I asked,

'What about? About us, the situation with Julia?'

'No', she said, 'Well, yes, kind of. You see, Jack, how can I tell you, I can't understand something, I'm all confused. Jack, God, I've got to tell you.'

So she told me. Hammer blow to the head. Hammer on the heart. Heart stopping wasn't the word for it. I got that bird-swallow choking feeling again. I was sure that if I opened my mouth, I'd spit out black tail feathers. She said,

'Jack, I saw Mo in Waitrose.'

I didn't know what to say, or what to think. I couldn't think. My head, my brain, seemed to stop working. I could only focus on making the tea. I made the tea. The thought of that other tea making came into my head. I wasn't using the china cups and saucers. I'd not used them since. Mugs were what I used now. I was quiet. Caroline was worried about the quiet. She shouldn't have been though, it was just how things were with me. She said

'Jack, you're very quiet, what do you think, how can I have seen Mo? Why did she think I had gone with Julia? What does it mean d'you think?'

I didn't reply. She wanted a reply, but I couldn't think of any words. I managed to say, without spitting bird feathers,

'Tea?'

And handed her a mug of tea. She seemed a bit annoyed then, but she took the tea anyway, said thanks and put it on the counter top. She said,

'Sod the sodding tea, look Jack, what the hell do you think is going on? Why did Julia tell everyone she was going on holiday with Mo, and tell Mo she was going away with me? What does it all mean? Do you think she suspected something, even though we'd not done anything? I just can't work it out, Jack, what's going on?'

I'd never had the urge to find meaning in stuff. This search for meaning people had was a bloody nightmare so far as I was concerned. Why couldn't people just accept that sometimes things were just the way they were, without any 'because'. What was wrong with people? No one tried to find meaning in trees, or grass, or birds. Well, maybe birds were a bit different, because I'd read about them being really dinosaurs, or had come from dinosaurs like in the Jurassic Park film, but that was science, that was different. All this meaning stuff was bollocks. There was a glimmer of hope here, though, I thought, just a glimmer. I had thought it was all crashing down around me, that I'd have to tell Caroline about what I'd done, that she'd then leave me, hate me. But here was a way out. She thought Julia had told Mo. She thought Julia had told me. Not that I had told anyone. Caroline wasn't thinking it was me. Not me. She didn't blame me. She wasn't thinking it was me that had made it up, but Julia. I said, 'Um, Caro, I dunno, where was it you saw Mo, and, um what did she say then exactly?'

'In Waitrose, I was totally, y'know, well, you can imagine, 'cause she asked me how was it in Turkey, and that she was surprised we were back so soon.'

'So what did you say?' asked Jack.

'What could I say?' replied Julia, running her hands through her hair.

'I was gobsmacked. I just said something or other, I can't remember, really, and got the hell out of there. I couldn't work it out, why she thought I'd gone to Turkey, but I couldn't say anything really because I'd no idea what was going on. I thought it best to just go along with it, y'know, 'till I could figure it out. Bloody Julia, what's she up to Jack? And, where is she if she's not in Turkey, not with me or Mo? And why say all that? And I'm feeding her bloody horses for God's sake. What a bloody cheek! And she's not with Pete either, unless he's in on it – that might be it! She might be trying to get at you, and has gone off with Pete, and she might have got him to pretend he didn't know where she was, but he did really. No, that can't be it, yes it might be, oh God, I'm confused. None of it makes sense does it?'

She was working it out in her head at the same time as talking to me, sort of talking out loud her thinking. I stayed quiet. Quiet was good, I thought, as I was not sure what to say, how to explain it, and the less I said the less chance I'd say something that would give it all away. I didn't usually talk my thinking, more thought about stuff, then talked. I wasn't really much of a talker anyway. More of a woman thing that was. Sometimes Bob and I could be together for hours, say at a cricket match or something, and we'd say nothing much to each other at all. Bob, mind, was more of a woman about it, because he would talk no end sometimes just like a turned on tap. Other times, like me, he'd be quiet and not talk at all. I didn't really want to talk about this with Caroline, but I had no choice. There she was, wanting to talk, wanting me to say something. I wanted to go out again, and walk, think about it, let it work through in my head. I answered Caroline,

'No, you're right, it doesn't make sense.'

But it did, of course, if only she knew. There we were drinking tea, with her puzzled over where Julia was, and Julia was right there in the garden. I couldn't let her go on thinking this could I? It was impossible. I wanted so much to tell her, but I didn't want to tell her at one and the same time. It would be the end of us. It was doing my head in. My head really hurt from it all. I suggested we went for a walk, so we finished our tea and went out along the lane down across the wheat field down to the brook. I usually took that walk alone, it was strange with Caroline beside me, strange but good. She talked about how she thought Julia had done the disappearing act on purpose, to wind me up. I agreed that was possible, but that she could have just gone away with Pete. Caroline reckoned Julia'd ditched Pete because he'd gone a bit far with the physical stuff, got a bit violent in the bedroom if I got her drift. Julia had told Caroline once or twice she and Pete had really gone for it, with ties and chains and stuff, and she'd got bruises to show in her private parts, and they were really bad, and that's why she'd not gone with him to Australia. Caroline said she hadn't told me the half of it, really, about that side of things, and how Julia treated Pete, as she'd seen his bruises too, but she reckoned they were well matched, and that they deserved each other but it still didn't explain her disappearance so far as Caroline was concerned. Of course it didn't.

My head was getting fuller and fuller from holding on to the story of Julia's disappearance. Bloody cow was bloody awful alive, bloody nightmare living with her, but Chrissake she was killing my head, killing me being dead. I agreed with Caroline that it didn't make sense, and that it was possible Pete and Julia had rowed, that Pete had maybe been violent to her, she to him, and that she'd gone off having invented the story of who she was going with, to maybe stop him going after her, to lay a kind of confusing trail. Pete had certainly seemed confused about where she was, and about how she was. Caroline wondered about Mo, that Julia didn't have to lie to her mother. Why do that? She said 'Maybe it wasn't her that told her mother, and what if,' she wondered out loud,

'What if Pete had done away with her, maybe that was it, he'd murdered her in a fit of jealous rage and then pretended she'd gone away with the others to cover his tracks, so one wouldn't question the other? Then he turned up at my house to make his story believable, like a kind of alibi. Wow! What about that? God, it doesn't bear thinking about, does it?'

She was so close to the truth, so close to home it hurt. I had to tell her, I had to.

'It's too farfetched,' I replied,

'Stay real Caro, c'mon let's get back. We're not going to work it out, are we?'

On the way back, we crossed back through the wheat field, up and over the common. Four or five crows were chasing away a buzzard, and when the job was done they swooped and fell to the trees. The dry, dead bracken crackled under our feet. New fern was pushing its way through. The shoots looked like those cleats I banged into the fence to thread wire through, only these were fat and green like short, stumpy, curled over fuses and I felt that if I just bent down and set light to them, I could set fire to the whole thing, let it all go up in flames, burn away, leave nothing alive behind.

As soon as we got back to the house, the phone rang. It was Mo. I mouthed to Caroline, 'it's Mo'. She understood, and went off to do something or other. Mo wanted to speak to Julia. I told her that Julia wasn't in. She barked her usual orders,

'So, where is she?'

'As if I would know', I replied.

'Tell her, tell her to call me. And tell her I can't get through to her mobile. Tell her, tell her I know.'

And she put the phone down. Bloody rude cow that she was. What the hell was that all about? I looked at Caroline, told her what Mo had said. Somehow, I felt as though I'd not just come into the house, but had come home. I felt so relaxed with Caroline being with me. She'd brought me in a glass of whisky, with ice. I'd no idea what time it was. We each took a sip of the whisky, I looked at her, she at me, and we went upstairs to bed.

19. It all comes out

It was very early. I looked at the clock. 5.30 am. Caroline was asleep but I was wide awake. I slipped out of bed, and went downstairs to make tea. It was a bright morning, it would be a good day, sunshine most probably, and warm. Next door's cockerel was calling away, bloody noisy thing that it was. It's not true what they say about dawn chorus, or at least it's true for birds but not for cockerels. Birds just do that thing when the sun comes up, but not cockerels. The bloody things crow all night and all day long. And what's more, they don't crow nicely, they crow like they are being strangled. People that go on about how great it is to live in the countryside ought to just adopt a cockerel. They'd soon see, or hear, and give it up altogether. I brought the tea up. Caroline stirred as I got back into bed. I had come to a decision. It was really hard. The question I'd been wrestling with was should I tell her, or should I not tell her. I was damned if I did, I was damned if I didn't. I had decided to tell her the truth. I couldn't go on any longer. I had one of those dreams again, only this time I had dreamt I was in Cornwall, and I'd finally made it. I'd escaped from everything, made a clean break and had managed to set up home there in a small house overlooking a river that led to the sea, and there was nothing between me and the wide open sea, I had such a sense of freedom, of complete peace. I figured that this was a sign that I should come clean, that my brain was working things out for me. I had to make an escape of sorts. The start of the escape was to come clean. I couldn't run away. The sense of my dream was one of relief. I woke completely relieved, as if I knew what it was I had to do. My brain had worked thing out, maybe. It was strange that dreams were always in pictures, that there was never any sound. They were vividly colourful but totally silent. Caroline was in the dream somewhere, or at least her hand was. I never saw her face in my dream or heard her voice. I had to tell her about Julia, about what had happened, I was sure about that. It was hard to stand back and just let her believe something that wasn't true. I couldn't do it. I had decided to take the risk and tell her.

She looked so peaceful lying there. Once I told her nothing would be the same again, ever. I said,
'Hey, Caro, here's your tea.'
She rolled toward me and opened her eyes. We'd made love last night, and in the morning light I could not believe how incredibly beautiful she was. I'd never felt this way for anyone ever before, never had these kind of feelings. I felt totally protective of her, and yet what I was thinking to say would be the one thing that

would hurt her. I so wanted not to hurt her, but I'd nowhere else to go, there was nothing else for it. I said,

'Caro, Caroline, I need to talk to you about something.'

She was awake and looking at me, although she hadn't lifted herself up. I went on,

'Caroline, it's about Julia. There's something I need to tell you.'

She asked me to wait a minute, got herself up level with me, rubbed her eyes, put her hands through her hair, and said,

'OK, so, Jack, what, what is it, what about Julia?'

I took a deep breath, I couldn't quite believe what I was doing. It was as if another me had taken over, while the real me was looking on from outside somewhere. I heard myself say,

'Caro, you know Julia's gone away, well, it's a bit more, um, it's a bit well, more complicated than that.'

I took another deep breath and continued. I told her about finding Julia in the bedroom, how she looked strange, and well, dead. I told her how I couldn't remember anything, and about the things Julia had done, how she had been with me. I didn't tell her about the name calling, that was too much, but I did tell her how Julia would thump and kick me, how any little thing would set her off. I thought that if I stopped talking, telling Caroline, that I'd not start again so I kept on, with the whole thing, that I thought I might have done something but I wasn't sure what, that I loved her – Caroline - that I couldn't bear keeping this all from her, that I had thought it was me that did it, how I had buried Julia in the compost, how it was all my fault for not being the man, but that it seemed like the right thing because everyone hated her and no one would mind that she was gone. In fact, everyone wanted her gone. I just couldn't remember, just didn't know what had happened, only that I'd had it in my head that one day I would stop her, and maybe that was the day. I stopped talking then, the flood subsided. I don't think I'd ever said so much in one go in my life.

Caroline did not say a word. She just looked at me, without moving, or saying anything. She said,

'You mean, Julia is.....Julia is....dead?'

'Yes, at least, well, yes.'

'And you, you mean, you think you did it?'

'Yes.'

She was looking at me all the time, frowning, her eyes wide, wide open. I could see she was trying to work it all out.

'But, all this time, you knew all this time? What about Turkey? You mean that was you? You made that up? And Pete, you let me think that.....'

I interrupted her,

'Caro, please, I just, I just couldn't lie to you any more, it just, well it seemed like the best thing at the time, I mean, Chrissake I can't remember what happened, it's been a nightmare.'

'You mean, you don't know if you, if you....God, I can't say the word, if you.....killed her?' she asked.

So I told her about finding Julia in the bedroom, this time in more detail, and she listened, and listened. She asked more questions as I went along, but she was patient and tried not to interrupt me. I told her everything, about the carpet, the phone, the jewellery and stuff, how I thought no one would miss Julia, she was like a plague for everyone, and since I'd found out about Bob, and stuff, how it was so much better that she was gone. She asked why I hadn't gone straight to the police. I said that it hadn't occurred to me, not that it was deliberate, but that I just had thought I could make Julia go away, that it was the simplest thing to do, I didn't really know what I was doing, and when I realised I should have gone to the police, it was too late, they'd not believe me, as she, Caroline, and I were an item, and they'd think I bumped off Julia to get her best friend, a sort of crime of passion sort of thing. She asked me again why I thought I had done it, got me to explain how I'd found Julia, what she looked like and that kind of thing. I couldn't really remember all of it, but I told her what I could. I didn't tell her about taking off Julia's clothes, or any of the dead body decomposing stuff, she would think me totally crazy. Maybe

I was crazy, I felt like I was losing it, losing my mind big time. It seemed like she was moving away from me. She asked me a few more questions I didn't have the answers to, how did I know it was me that did it, could something else have happened, how could it have been me? I just could not remember. Right then, with her asking me, in the middle of it all, I don't know why but I started to sob, great heavy shudders like before, great gulping sobs. All I could think was that I'd lost her, lost my beautiful, clever, Caroline. She would never love me, could never love me. What the hell had I done? And why had I thought things could work out any differently? It was all a mess, a great fucking, sodding mess, and I had made it so. It was all my fault, all mine. Fucked up marriage, fucked up home, fucked up friendship with Bob, fucked up with Caroline. I was sodding useless. Fucked up my life, fucked up my head. Julia was right, what sort of a man was I? Not a man at all. Jacky, fucking useless Jacky. I think I must have spoken some of this out loud, as I could hear myself muttering, with words coming out as sort of jerky howls. Caroline slid across the bed to me, and put her arms around me. She put her arms around me, and held me close to her. I felt her do that, felt her warmth, heard her voice. She sounded so calm, so very calm. I gave up then, gave in to her, gave up to thinking nothing at all, and everything seemed to fold in and go dark as she shushed me, and said it would be all right, over and over she said that it would be all right. But it could never be all right, not ever.

20. Borrowing

Bob had woken up bright and early, and he was determined to show off to Dianne just what he could do in the garden. He felt like the king of the hill, top of the heap, fantastic, never better. He had told Jack about Julia and had survived that, they were still friends, and that would work out. Dianne had let him stay at her place overnight for the first time, she'd got more comfortable with him and her, and with her boys. Everything was going to work out. Today he was going to make a start on the vegetables. He knew Jack had a rotivator, Jack would let him borrow that, and then he was going to make the patch at the top of Di's garden into a vegetable plot. He'd suggested it to Di, and she'd been quite keen. Actually, she'd said she didn't mind, which wasn't keen exactly, but it wasn't no. All he needed to do was mark it out, rotivate it, and give it a good bit of help with some decent compost, potash and the like, and he was sure Jack wouldn't mind if he had some of his compost, the good rotted down stuff at the back. Jack'd got plenty. Bob made a good start with marking it all out, using string and pegs and the two boys helped, and got in the way, then helped, then got bored, and went off on their bikes. Bob missed his girls, remembering that Susie had been a bitch in a way with access. She always made out that he had to stick to the routine of every two weeks, then changed it all when she wanted to, to suit what she was up to. When he suggested a change, which was rare, she went ape, said he wasn't taking his responsibilities seriously. She had the upper hand there and no mistake. Still, at least they were still talking, or sort of talking, and he did see a lot of the girls but it wasn't ideal in his flat. It wasn't too bad while they were little but he really had to think about a bigger place and he thought that Di's place would be ideal with the big house, and big garden. She might let him move in, if he played his cards right, not that it was about cards, as he really did love Di. She'd had a hard time of it with her ex, and she needed a bit of TLC. She was a very special woman, Di. Just as he had finished marking out the plot, the sky went all dark, and busted open and huge drops of rain came flying down so hard they bounced off the path. Bugger he thought and realised that he should have looked at the weather forecast. He ran inside and looked over at Di who was in the kitchen with a 'told you so' sort of look on her face. She'd made two cups of coffee and Bob wondered why it was that women always knew what was going to happen. They talked a lot, he knew that, maybe that was it, and all the talk was about what had happened, and knowing what had happened meant they knew what would happen. They sure figured things out. Always knew what men were thinking, at least Susie did, and Di seemed to be able to figure him out really easily, she could predict what he was going to say. Sometimes he didn't have to say anything. Susie used to say, for example,

'I know what you're going to say, you're going to say blah blah blah………..'

And she would come out with it. And she'd would be right, and he would stay quiet, because she'd said it all, so why say anything. And then she'd say,

'So, say something, why don't you? Aren't you interested in us, in our marriage, or what? Obviously you're not, otherwise you'd say something.'

But what was there to say? She'd already said it all. Di wasn't like that, or she was a bit. She would tell him she knew what he was thinking, but she wouldn't say it for him. She said he was as easy to read as graffiti on a ladies' bog wall, and what that was meant to mean, he didn't know as he'd never seen what was written on a ladies' bog wall, and he'd no intention of finding out. What he did know was that he hated playing games, and Di wasn't a game player. She gave it to him straight, she did, like that first time, when he and she got together. He'd known her for a while from visiting at Jack's and he'd always thought she was a bit struck on Jack and she'd been over to give Jack some eggs, and he'd arrived just as she was leaving, and she'd mentioned she had a blocked drain, and Jack said he'd call round later to see if he could fix it. Bob didn't want to stray onto Jack's ground, if he fancied Di, but Jack had never mentioned it, so Bob'd got his drain rods in the back of the car, and said it was no problem to pop round and help out. Straight away Jack said that in that case, he'd leave it to Bob, then, so if Jack had had any sort of thing for Di, Bob was sure he would have warned him off. It was a clear sign to Bob that Jack was saying 'Go on matey boy, she's all yours.' So Bob went next door with his drain rods, and Di's drain was well and truly blocked. He found half a house brick in the bottom of the drain, and all sorts of gunk, explaining to Di as he went how it built up, if you didn't watch what you put down the kitchen sink, in a nice way, not patronising like he knew some blokes were to women, telling her that fat and grease and stuff, it goes down in what you think is liquid, but it goes all solid, like, and builds up, and before you know it, bang, or block was more like it. Di laughed at his joke, even though he hadn't meant it as a joke. He didn't really do funny like some blokes he knew. Anyhow, she'd invited him in for a cuppa, and before he knew what he was doing he had invited her out for a drink. Over the drink she'd said,

'Look, Bob, I don't go out with blokes a lot, and I don't mess around. I've got two boys and they come first, but I do like you, and I'd like it if we saw each other again, all right?'

Yes, Bob thought, that was very all right. Di was all woman, big and beautiful. He knew she wasn't every bloke's cup of tea, but she was fabulously big breasted, big hearted, big bummed. All over big and he loved that, and it meant that when they were in bed together, he could grab her bum and pull her towards him, and bury his head in her breasts, so that he almost suffocated in her.

'What a way to go,' he joked. She laughed too. She said he made her laugh. It wasn't intentional, not that. He didn't have to try with Dianne, it just came out like that, which meant he could be himself, and not have to try. It was so easy with her, and she said he made her feel a million, like a real woman. She'd started wearing low cut things again, and said how he had made her feel all sexy, being wanted in the way he wanted her, in the way she wanted him. He was really glad that she'd packed in smoking, really glad as he hadn't wanted to wake up one day and find himself kissing what looked like a cat's bottom.

Bob could never understand what Jack had seen in Julia, for example she was far too skinny, all skin and bones, and you couldn't snuggle down on a cold night with a bird like that. Bird. That was Julia, he thought, like a scrawny bird, she was, all beak and no feathers, no flesh either, and what he'd been thinking of he couldn't say or explain. Mind, he had been drunk at the time, and lonely, and when you're in that sort of mind even tits like that were welcome, even tits like poached eggs but what a bloody mistake, and bloody hell he'd regretted it ever since.

He'd had to make out to the others that he didn't go for Di, because of Julia's bloody attitude, and because Di's ex might get to hear which he did feel bad about, but as they'd got together more, Di's ex was less of an issue, okay a bit worrying because he was a big bloke, and unpredictable, but less of an issue for him and Di. It was Di's boys that were more the problem. She was very protective of them, that was understandable and she didn't want them to get to know someone, to then be disappointed. She was careful like that and Bob respected her for it but she needn't have worried, though because she could trust him, and she just needed a bit of time to know she could trust him. He wasn't like her ex, what was his name, Steve. Bob didn't play away. Bastard. How could he do that to Di? It was a shame he was six feet three inches tall, and built, otherwise Bob would have told him a thing or two, yes he bloody well would. Steve had seven inches on Bob. Not that height was an issue for Bob, no, he'd have given Steve a run for his money. Bob did feel a bit sensitive about his waistline, though, because he was carrying a bit more there than he'd have liked. Bit more on top wouldn't have hurt either. Steve had a temper on him by all accounts, although Bob had never met him but he knew him by reputation and it was a bloody good job he'd upped sticks away from round here, Bob was relieved about that. Steve did want to see the boys though, to his credit, but that caused a bit of a problem because he'd never stick to the rules and there was no telling when he'd turn up. Di had been to the police, and got a court agreement about access and everything, but it was hard to prove stuff that happened, and it got really, really tiring. Last time Steve'd been around was just before Di took the kids on holiday. He'd just turned up, said he wanted to see the boys. Di had argued with him, said he couldn't, that they had an agreement as to where and when, under supervision, but he wouldn't have it, so she said she'd call the police and he'd stormed off.

Bob liked it at Di's. He felt at home there, like it was home, and it didn't feel like he was stepping into her life, more that they were making a life together, so he didn't feel like an intruder. She had this way of things, a way that made him feel part of things, which was funny, as with Susie in the last year or more that they were together he'd felt like he was a visitor in his own home, like she was all polite to him, and distant, like he had just come from next door to borrow something, as if it wasn't really his home at all. They had talked about it, and he had said he felt more like her friend, it was as if they were friends sharing a house, not like a married couple and she asked him what he thought living like a married couple would be like, and then she reeled off a few things to make the point that he wasn't up to the mark and Bob couldn't say anything to that. She seemed to have it all worked out, so from then on in, Bob felt like he was on borrowed time, like he would be given his notice at any moment. He had never felt more unwanted in his life, it reminded him of the time at school, when he'd been walking home one time, and some of the boys in the class had been after him. They'd been teasing him for being fat, called him 'fattie', and 'shortass'. It had gone on for ages. He'd laughed it off, but this time on the way home they were shoving and pushing him. He didn't know what to do, really. That's when Jack had appeared, on his bike, and told them to leave him alone. He was a lot bigger than them, but he could have just ridden on by as he and Jack weren't friends or anything. They called him names too, after that. 'Fatty friend' was one, but Jack didn't seem to care. He didn't seem to need friends. Jack was taller, and more well-built than the others in the year, probably from all the work on the farm, as Bob found out later. Bob nodded thanks to him, Jack nodded back. They didn't speak then, they didn't speak about that ever again, but the boys left Bob alone, and Jack and Bob struck up a sort of friendship.

Bob could see a time in the not too far future, when he would have the girls at Di's, with Di's boys. They weren't too far away in age, and he was sure they would get on together in a sort of boys-hate-girls-hate-boys kind of way. That was the next step, to get the kids together, then who knows, Di might even make an honest man of him. He was a bit worried about Steve though. It would be better, just perfect if he wasn't about, but then there was always something to make things less than perfect. Life couldn't just be easy could it, there always had to be something. Steve was his something.

21. More borrowing

Caroline had got dressed, and was in the kitchen sorting out some breakfast. She'd left Jack upstairs in a deep sleep. He obviously needed that. He hadn't been able to say much more, and there was so much more she needed to know. After he'd stopped sobbing, he'd fallen totally to sleep. She was worried about him and deeply concerned about what had happened. Jack didn't seem to know what had actually happened. Caroline didn't know what to make of it. She didn't know if he had done it or not. She knew a bit about male violence, and domestic violence, even violent women in relationships. She'd no idea that it had been that bad between him and Julia, or that Julia could have been that bad towards Jack, even though she did play around a lot. It had been like that from the start, she had warned Jack. He must have known what she was like when he married her. It did make sense, though, she could see how it might have happened. There were a few pieces of it that made sense, for example, if it had been like that all those years, it could have been something of a trigger, something Julia said that made Jack explode. The straw that broke the camel's back. Something said or done once too often, and the explosion followed.

She couldn't really understand why Jack had put up with it all those years. If it had been that bad, why not get divorced? What did Julia get out of it? What did either of them get out of it? Mind, she also knew that in situations like that, there was a kind of co-dependency, that two people could sort of exist side by side, in a 'better the devil you know' kind of relationship where getting out was far more complex and difficult than just putting up with. She thought about herself, her own actions. She blamed herself for not seeing this, it was kind of inevitable, really. If she could have a wish it would be to have the gift of hindsight, and always see things twenty-twenty. So many things were only clear when you looked back. She felt that she should have done something, way before now, instead of it all unravelling like this. She should have, could have talked to Julia. God, Julia. Could she really be dead? Caroline couldn't believe it. Dead, out there, in the compost. Surely not. It couldn't be true. Had it all been a bad dream, a nightmare? Was any of it real? She wasn't sure what real was, or whether Jack, in his current state could tell fact from fiction. What if he'd invented it all, and it was, for example, possible, that he could have imagined it. He seemed really close to the edge, maybe he'd gone over the edge? But if he had, that did not explain where Julia was.

She wasn't sure what to do. She could go to the police maybe, go with Jack to see his GP maybe, talk to Bob maybe, to Mo. No, not Mo. She'd go ape. She wasn't capable of seeing things rationally. Mind, nor was Bob really. What about Dianne. She'd known Jack for years, and was quite close as neighbours go. She was closer to him than most would be, and she was level headed. What sort of raving loony would she think Caroline was, if she went round there and started on about Jack having killed Julia. There was only one person, she thought, who would really be bothered about Julia, and that was Mo. Caroline couldn't believe how hard hearted she was in thinking that. The woman she'd known all these years, and she didn't care at all that she was dead. At least, she did care in a way. She thought it was an awful thing that Julia was dead, but she had no feelings about Julia being dead, in fact, Caroline felt a sense of relief, yes, relief, that was it, she was relieved. It meant not facing Julia about her and Jack, no divorce, nothing like that. No more talks about men, the many blokes she'd seen and had sex with. It was sex with Julia, or so she said, that she never fell in love with any of them, and she would laugh and tell Caroline how easy it was to fool men, how she liked to bed them and break their hearts. Pete had been a bit different, though, but even so she would not even let him in, as whatever feelings Julia had, she kept them buried down deep, under lock and key, and no one got in there, not even Caroline.

But how could she and Jack possibly manage to keep Julia's death a secret. How? It just wasn't possible. The fact that Jack thought it was, was madness. Caroline was amazed she was thinking this way. Maybe Jack had infected her, with his same kind of madness.

Sitting there in the kitchen, staring out at the garden, she thought it could all be done, they could keep Julia's death a secret between them, her and Jack. But it was all wrong, wrong, and they should come clean and tell the police. If Jack had done it, he would be put in prison, she would wait for him. Yes, they should come clean. She thought about Jack. He had killed her then, killed Julia. Not intentional of course, and it hadn't changed how she felt about him. She loved him. This that he had told her had not changed a thing. She felt so protective towards him, wanted to make everything all right for him. Maybe they could keep Julia's death a secret. There was always Pete. They could tell Mo that Julia had gone to Australia with Pete. She'd be suspicious, she'd want to talk to Julia. Of course she would. Could they do it, keep it secret from Mo? It would buy some time, maybe to allow them to think about stuff. Maybe she and Jack could go to Australia, start a new life together. No. It would all come out and someone would come after them. She had a strong sense of justice, and this wasn't the way. They couldn't bury it, as it would always be there. And anyway, if Julia was buried in the garden, someone would buy this place and find her. No, they had to stay put, figure something out. She drank her tea and watched the rain drops run down the window, running into each other. She remembered the raindrop race game she had played with her sister as a girl. They would each choose a rain drop and see whose would get to the bottom first, over and over they'd play that and it didn't seem to matter who won. When they got bored with that, they'd breathe on the window and with their fingers draw stick men and faces on the steamed up panes. Silly how those small, insignificant memories came back at the oddest times, connected with nothing, they just appeared from somewhere in the way back.

There was a knock at the back door. It was Bob.

'Hiya Caroline, um, just wondered like, if I could borrow Jack's rotivator, y'know just for today? Looks like rain's clearin' up?'

Caroline was jolted back to reality. Bob.

'Um, well, Jack's still in bed, he's um, not feeling very well.'

She made that up, but it was sort of true. He wasn't well. She continued,

'I don't know about the rotivator, do you want me to ask him and let you know?'

He said,

'Um. Well, okay then, but, um, I'd like to get on with it today, like, y'know, so I'll pop back if that's alright, if I ain't disturbing you. Needn't be any bother as I know where he keeps it. I'll pop back then, bit later, or he can let me know if he likes, I'll be next door at Di's today, okay?'

He had a sort of knowing grin on his face. 'Cheeky sod,' Caroline thought, and replied,

'Yeah, okay, Bob, yeah no problem I should imagine, but I'll pass the message on, ask him, okay? Thanks then, see ya.'

Speaking normally to him was a real effort. The normal day-to-day had come crashing through into the weird and not very normal. What if he knew, she wondered, what would Bob think, or say, if he knew.

Upstairs, Jack was stirring. He blinked in the light and asked Caroline was time it was, and then said,

'Bloody hell fire', when she told him, and,

'Why didn't you wake me? I never stay in bed this late, well not usually.'

She told him she hadn't had the heart to wake him, and that in her opinion he badly needed to sleep. He told her he was really glad she was still there, that he'd thought she'd leave him, go to the police or some such thing.

'No, Jack, I'd not do that. But we do need to talk about it, what we do now, y'know, we can't keep it secret. We have to get it sorted out. It might not have been you, did you think about that? It might have been............'

'Yeah? Been who? There's no other bugger, is there? I'm the one, I can't see who else. There was no one else, at least not that I saw. Plenty as'd've wanted to mind.'

Caroline agreed.

'Well, okay, so, well, it still might have been someone else, just because you didn't see anyone – you were in the workshop anyhow. I don't know.' She sighed, and paused, before continuing.

'Anyway it was an accident wasn't it. You didn't mean to do it, even if it was you, did you? I mean, you could argue it was an accident, people would understand, you know, in the circumstances.'

Jack looked at her, he looked horrified, he said,

'I'm not going to tell all that, Caro, I can't. Tellin' you is one thing, but telling all that to other people, strangers, I can't Caro, I just can't. She can stay dead and buried, and good bloody riddance. No one will miss her, we can make out that she's gone off with that Pete, maybe. I had thought Turkey, but that's a bit farfetched. Australia is a bit more believable, like. No one will know, we can do it, mind, we'll have to figure out Mo. She is a bit of a problem, but she'll believe us, we'll make her believe us.'

Caroline looked at Jack. He was in a bad way. This was his dead wife's mother he was talking about, pretending Julia was still alive to Mo. It wasn't on, was it? She did think that it might work, though, to pretend Julia was dead. She'd believed it herself, so why not? Maybe Jack had had more practice at this than she had, he'd been doing it for a while now, but it didn't sit well with her. She tried to convince him, and herself at the same time,

'It's not right Jack, it's just not right, it'll all come out, don't you see, we can't keep it quiet, people will ask questions. There will be too many questions.'

The more she said and the more she argued the case to come clean, the more she wanted to just bury it all, cover it up. She thought about the awfulness of what would come. Mo would find out Julia was dead and that she'd been lied to, there would be questions, the police. It would mean going to court, Jack arrested, Jack going to prison. Their whole lives would never be the same again. All because of Julia. She was dead but was more trouble dead than she had been alive. Caroline didn't think that was possible, but here they were, agonising over what to do, just like Jack had probably agonised over what to do about Julia and him when she was alive. All those years married to her, and the things he'd put up with. Caroline had never thought people deserved to die, but maybe Julia was an exception, and Julia wasn't going to get the better of them, dead though she was. She wasn't going to ruin their future. Maybe it could work to keep it quiet, even for a bit while they talked it over. Maybe they had to make it work. She said this to Jack. She said,

'Why don't we not do anything just now, there's no rush, let's think about what to do for the best, eh, talk some more later.'

That was good for Jack, she knew he liked to think quietly and not talk, but he didn't at all seem to mind her nattering away. She thought how different it must be for him, from what he'd told her completely different from the way it was, living with Julia. And now she was dead.

Caroline had brought Jack up a mug of tea, and they fell silent then, each to their own thoughts, he drinking his tea, she with her head on his shoulder, his strong arm around her. Both were thinking in the quiet of what was left of the morning. Caroline was also thinking about the fact that Jack had lied to her, too. She could see why, understand it even, but it didn't feel good knowing he had lied to her along with the others – Mo, Bob, Dianne, and Pete. She could only think that he must have been desperate, and very alone. At least he had her now, and together they would do the right thing. She was sure of that.

Bob came back later and this time Jack was out of bed, showered, and dressed. He and Caroline had a late breakfast – she called it brunch – and she'd gone off to do something to do with work, counselling appointment she'd said. Bob was full of beans, wanted to borrow the rotivator, which was fine, Jack said, for as long as he liked, no rush as Jack hadn't got any more to do for a bit. Bob knew where it was, so that was all right, he could help himself, Jack said. Bob was back to his usual self, carried on about what a bloody nonsense it was about Beckham back in the England side, and what a show Vaughanie put up at Headingly, eh? He wanted to know if Jack had changed his mind at all about the Windies next year. Jack had not.

'You make your own luck in cricket, that's certain,' said Bob, going on as usual not waiting for a reply or anything from Jack. 'It's destiny, y'see, he was intended to do them runs, it was him that made his own luck. Perfection. He never put a foot wrong all innings. It was meant to happen.'

He went on about the football then.

'That bloody Maclaren what's he playin' at, eh? What a tosser. It needs young blood does that team, young ones with talent, not oldies like Becks. He's past it, that's what 'e is. Thirty two bloody years old he is. Most others'd be retired by now. Is he playing safe or what? He's mad, he needs to think ahead, that's what I'd do, think ahead, and get young players in the team now, ready for the next world cup. Beckham won't be able to play then. Mac's too much thinking about the present. He must think Beckham a bloody lucky charm or summat, eh Jack, what do you reckon?'

He paused for breath and realised, at last, that Jack had been quiet.

Jack replied,

'Um, yeah, lucky charm right enough, maybe it will work.'

Then Bob said,

'By the way, mate, um, can you borrow me some of your compost, you know, the old stuff, the real rotted down stuff? I can call round with the barrow later if you like.'

And Bob thought Jack had an odd look on his face just then. But went off whistling something, not a tune exactly, just aimless, happy, whistling.

22. Julia goes to Australia

It had been great having Caro with me. I felt so much better. I felt I could breathe, as if some great pressing thing on my chest had been lifted away. Things were going to work out, I could feel it. I couldn't leave it to chance like Caro was suggesting. Together we could make our own luck. We could pull off the Julia thing, I was sure of it. It would take us both being brave, both wanting it to happen. We could do it.

Then Bob. Bob had this way, sometimes, of hitting on the very thing, without realising it. He'd put his finger on it this time. He turned up, asked about the compost, and everything closed in again. Chrissakes why that of all bloody things, and why now? I felt sick. My stomach turned over, disappeared into my shoes, and went somewhere beyond. Bob didn't seem to notice my reaction, which was just as well. So, he wanted compost. Not any old compost, but the compost at the back, the rotted stuff, the stuff where Julia was buried in the carpet. By now she'd be well cooked, I thought. Not quite cheese exactly, but cooked enough. Chrissakes, what the hell did he want compost for. I could get it for him. That would stop him getting it, but he would want to help. Help. Christ. I wished Caroline was here, she'd know what to do. Bob, bloody hell, Bob and his sodding gardening. He wasn't even much good at it. I had to think. My head was hurting again. I thought I could do it, thought it would be all right, that we just had Julia to sort out. Now this. I couldn't say no to Bob, I just couldn't. I didn't even think it funny that he wanted to borrow the compost. Borrow it. As if he could give it back to me when he'd done with it. Fat chance. When he asked me, I just nodded, a bit stunned, I said,

'Yeah, okay mate, whatever,' and off he went.

Said he'd be back with his wheelbarrow. Shit. I realised that I'd have to get in first. I couldn't let him help himself out there. He'd find her. I ran over to the shed, unlocked it, and got my barrow out. I got the rotivator out ready, then I took the rotivator round to Di's place and knocked on the door. He answered, pleased as anything, said he'd leave the compost until next day, do the rotivating first, and then get stuck in. I told him no need, that I'd sort out a few barrowfuls. He was keen to help, but I said I could bring it over barrow load by barrow load, and he could be digging it in, many hands make light work sort of thing. Di overheard this and agreed. So that was that, disaster averted. I did then think that maybe Bob wouldn't mind Julia being dead. Maybe it would make his life easier, but he had a gob on him the size of the channel tunnel, so couldn't see how he would keep shtum about it. I would talk to Caroline about it later, see what she reckoned.

The phone rang when he got back to the house. It was Mo. She was worried about Julia.

'Jack, Mo. Julia not in then?'

She'd not replied to any of the mobile messages Mo had left her. Mo was pretty annoyed, and a bit worried.

'Where is the damned girl?' she asked.

'Dunno,' I replied, I was frantic. I hadn't expected Mo to call again so soon, and I wasn't sure at all what to say.

'Give me Caroline's number, Jack, I don't seem to have it. I'll call her, maybe she knows. And did you give her my message?'

I had to say no, that I hadn't seen Julia. As for Caro's number, what could I do? I couldn't give her Caro's number. I said,

'Mo, look, um, I can't seem to lay my hands on it just now, the whatsit, address book has gone walkabout, I'll find it and call you back, okay?'

'Fine, call me back. If she does turn up, tell her, no don't bother I'll tell her myself.'

And she was gone. And so was I. I threw myself onto the sofa and buried my head in the cushions. I heard myself making that moaning noise again. I beat the side of the sofa over and over with my fists. What the hell could I do about Mo? If only she weren't around, I thought, everything would be perfect, just perfect. Damn, bloody damn, bloody damnation, bloody damn her to hell and her bloody daughter I hoped she was rotting in hell or if there was a place worse, let her be rotting there. I punched the sofa over and over, then, slowly, stopped. There had to be some way of getting Mo out of the way, or putting her off somehow. It couldn't last though. What could we do? No, what could I do. It had to be me. I shouldn't have dragged Caroline into all this. It was my fault. She was blameless. It had to be me that sorted this one out. I had to get Mo to think Julia had gone away. Julia had to go somewhere and stay there forever. Not Turkey, maybe Australia? I could tell Mo that Julia had gone after Pete. Yes, that would work. I didn't want to drag Pete into it, though, poor bugger, but that was his lookout. Mo might want his contact details, but I could deal with that, keep her fed snippets and stuff. After all, I didn't even know the guy's proper name. Yes, that would work, Julia could go to Australia after Pete. Then I had a thought. What if, what if Mo had an accident? Could that be the answer? I was stunned with myself that I could think such a thing, but somehow it seemed logical. With her out of the way….no it bloody didn't, Chrissakes, what was I thinking? I had to stop all of it, just stop.

23. Mo Goes to Australia

Mo was worried about her daughter. She knew Julia had found out about her and Pete. She had no idea that Pete and Julia were, or had been, an item. It had been a complete accident that she'd met him, one night in a pub, that was all it was, a night out, and there he was, at the bar. He made a pass and before she knew it she'd invited him back to her place, and they were in bed together. It was fast and furious. She'd been flattered, it was uncomplicated, and she thought never to see him again, really. It was a convenience for both of them, nothing more. She had seen him again, always it was for sex. No one else knew. He had no idea she was Julia's mother, and she'd no idea he was Julia's lover as well. They'd found out by chance. Stupid really. He'd come back to England and called her up. Said this was his last visit and would she see him? She would, she was excited to see him or rather, was excited at the thought of having him, physically. After all, what fifty something woman normally had a man of his age. He was gorgeous. Rugged, with a taught, muscular body, and he didn't want anything else. But that last visit to her house, they were lying in bed together and he'd seen a photo next to her bed, one she'd recently put there. He asked her if it was her, and she'd said it was her daughter, Julia. He'd been totally shocked.

'Julia, um, Julia? Is she, um, is she married?'

She laughed, and said,

'Yes, why are you in the market? She is, of sorts, to a bloke she doesn't exactly see eye to eye with, and God knows why she stays with him, or he with her, but anyway, yes she is.'

'And, her married name, what would that be, then?'

'Um, it's Carver, Julia Carver. Her husband is Jack Carver.'

Mo thought she saw a flicker of something in his eyes, but she couldn't be sure. She really didn't know him very well. Then he rolled her towards him, kissed her on the mouth very hard, and she felt him want her again, and she him. Fast, hard, furious, she thought it was as if he was making the most of it, as if it might be his last time. She knew he was going back to Australia and he'd said he would most likely not be back, and she didn't care. He was there with her now, he was hard and real, and very, very male, and she loved that. Even so, she'd be glad when he went. She didn't want any man sticking around in her life. Mo had her life just the way she wanted it. Men were in when she wanted them in, and they were out in the same way.

Afterwards, Pete felt drained. All this time he'd been fucking Julia's mother. Her fucking mother and he'd not even realised it. There was something about her, he knew that, but her mother? It felt quite weird somehow, quite a turn on and he'd fucked Mo hard when he'd found out, out of frustration, to get back at Julia, the bitch, she was a bitch, she'd kept him at arm's length all these years. Bitch. So he'd screw her mother, and screw her, teach Julia a lesson. And then, he'd tell Julia exactly what he'd done, what her mother had done with him, how they'd enjoyed each other on and off, how her mother knew how to pleasure him. Yes. He'd do that and she could see how it felt to be screwed. He'd see the look on her face, see her shocked, and disbelieving. And then he'd go back to Australia, for good and get on with his life.

Pete thought he should tell Mo about Julia as he wanted them both to know and it would be part of burning bridges. He would let them burn, let them both bloody well burn, so he told Mo that he thought he knew her daughter. She was surprised, asked him how that was, and so he told her about the diving, and that Julia and he had been an item for a while. She was suddenly more interested, and asked,

'An item? What do you mean an item?'

'You know, we knew each other, sort of were seeing each other.'

Of course, Mo wanted to know in what way, so Pete told her.

'In the usual way,' and winked.

Mo was lost for words, but managed to ask,

'Was this, is this, well, recent?'

'Yep, luv, we've seen each other recently, and yes, before you ask, in that sort of way.'

Mo wanted him to leave. She felt awful. Used. Dirty, somehow. It wasn't right, her daughter and Pete, and herself and Pete. How was it possible? She couldn't believe it and she should make him leave, of course, but then he was leaving anyway, and it was too late for that and what was done was done but what a bloody awful mess. She said,

'You're a bastard, aren't you? A bloody bastard. Does Julia know?'

'No, not yet.'

'What do you mean, not yet, you mean, don't tell me you're thinking of telling her?'

'That's right, I think I might well.'

Mo tried to persuade him out of it.

'Don't please, you shouldn't, don't, please Pete. It'll, well it won't get any of us anywhere will it, I mean, it's not worth it is it? What good would it do? Why upset things?'

Pete looked at Mo. She really was a fine looking woman. However, now that he looked at her closely her saw how much of Julia was in her, or rather, realised how much Julia was like her which was possibly why he had been drawn to her when they first met. He wasn't that much of a bastard, but he couldn't help himself. Julia bloody well deserved it, and she'd been enough of a bad girl. They'd both liked that side of each other. His personal life had been ruined by her really, he couldn't be with anyone else, not properly, all because of her, didn't really want anyone else so she should be punished and they'd both enjoy that. Yes he would tell her, he would tell her he'd been bad, that he'd been a really bad boy. He said,

'Look, Mo, see it's like this, I'm not going to tell her, okay? At least, I'm going back home, and I will most likely see her one last time, and if it comes up it comes up. If it doesn't, it doesn't.'

He left her guessing, but Mo knew that he would tell Julia. Deep down she just knew it. She felt awful, but she just couldn't see how to stop it unravelling and this left her feeling completely helpless.

And it had come up of course. Pete'd made sure of that. But it had only come up after he'd taken Julia to bed. He screwed her hard, and she loved it, harder still, and she loved that, and in the middle of it all, he told her.

Mo called Jack again.

'Caroline's number?'

Jack said,

'Sorry, um, Mo I don't have it here, can't find the book, you know, the address thing.'

'Never mind then, I, um. Well, How was Julia when you saw her, did she mention me or anything like that?'

Mo didn't usually really talk to Jack let alone quiz him about Julia but she needed to know if Julia was mad with her, avoiding her. He replied,

'Um, well, I haven't really seen her, so I can't say, sorry.'

'Fine, well, call me when you find it.'

She put the phone down. It was obvious to Mo that Julia was avoiding her. She'd been avoiding her for days. She even seemed to have convinced Jack to lie for her. Julia was up to something. There was something wrong and Mo knew what it was. She knew that finding out about her and Pete had probably meant the end of the mother-daughter thing, such as it was. She needed to talk to Julia, tell her it was all mistake, an accident, nothing more. She hadn't intended to go to bed with her daughter's lover. It had just happened like that, and she didn't even know he had taken Julia to bed as well. Julia had never even mentioned him. Mind, she never talked about men with her, not even Jack. Julia had always blamed her for the thing with her father. Not that Mo knew about that until it was far, far too late. And this Pete, this would have been a fling, an affair or something. What if Jack found out? No wonder Julia'd kept it quiet. What if it was more serious? Had she messed things up for her daughter? Surely not. It couldn't be serious, Julia couldn't possibly be getting serious with a man like

Pete. He clearly couldn't be trusted, and anyway, he was going back to Australia for good. A thought struck her then. Julia wasn't around at the moment. Had she? No. Surely she couldn't have? How could she, Mo, have been so stupid. The thought struck Mo that maybe, just maybe, Julia might just have left Jack, and gone after Pete. Silly bitch that she was, she might just have done it. Mo had to speak to Caroline. Caroline would know. She'd have to be careful, though, as Caroline would know about Pete and Julia, but hopefully not about her and Pete unless Julia had confided in her. She would have to sound out Caroline carefully, that's if Caroline would talk to her. Go carefully. Yes, that was it. Carefully.

24. At Caroline's

I couldn't wait for Caroline to come back. Normally, I would go for a walk, think about stuff, let the walking and the fields soak me up and somehow the answers would come. Not this time. This time, I needed Caroline. I got in the car and drove to her place. When I knocked on the door, she opened it, and I fell into her arms. I felt so tired, and so weak, as if somehow all the energy had been sucked out of me. I didn't understand how that could be possible. I was strong, hell I was stronger than anyone I knew. I was well built, muscles in all the right places Caroline said. Well, even so, if you'd pushed me with your little finger, I'd have fallen over. That's what I felt like. Caro had some music on, some woman singing like a wailing cat. Caroline said it was from a film called Diva, more properly it was from something called La Wally, but she had the film sound track. I thought 'right wally' was more like it, but as Caroline was pouring me a drink, I sat and listened. It was incredibly sad. I don't know if it was because I felt so weak, it must have been, but I felt the prick of tears starting in my eyes. I'd never rated opera stuff, thought it all a bit of nonsense all them heaving bosoms on stage, and when they were dying they sang even more loudly. If they'd had that much energy they shouldn't be dying. I didn't hold with singing stuff when it could be perfectly well said instead, and anyway you could never work out what they were singing as it was always Italian or some such foreign stuff. But this, this that Caroline had on was different somehow. Somehow it got right to me. Maybe I'd been missing something. She came back then, and said how pleased she was to see me, that she'd been just about to set off for my place. I had to tell her, about Mo and what she'd said about Julia which I thought was odd as she never really spoke to me, and about Bob and the compost, and how I was worried he'd dig up Julia. So I did. And the Wally music played away in the background and it was okay really, not bad at all. And Caroline listened to me, and didn't say anything until I'd finished. And then she said,

'Well, Mo rang me earlier.'

Well, you could have blown me away then, one puff and I'd have been gone.

'What do you mean? I didn't give her your number! How did she, well, how..........?'

Caroline continued,

'She said she hoped I didn't mind her ringing, but she'd found my number jotted down on a note she'd been left by Julia. Actually, Jack, she came over.'

'What!' I exclaimed, 'What was she doing coming over here to see you? What did she want?'

'Well, you know, that's where it gets really interesting. She wanted to know if I knew where Julia was, and if I thought Pete had anything to do with it. She also wanted to know if Julia had confided in me. I asked her about what, and she said, well, about anything private, about private stuff, anything about herself, maybe, for example, if Julia had said anything about her and any men friends. Honestly, Jack I didn't know what to say, or what she was on about. I was so worried anyway about you know, about Julia being dead, and being face to face with her, I should have told her I wasn't going to be in, but I didn't think quickly enough. Honestly, Jack, it was a nightmare. I told her that I didn't really know anything, but that I had seen Pete – I couldn't lie to her about that – and that you'd seen Pete too. She got all worked up then, and asked me was that amicable, between you and him. I said sort of, in the circumstances, and she got all agitated again then and said she should go, but she asked me did I think Julia had followed Pete to Australia. I said I didn't know, that I really didn't know, that she hadn't said anything to me about any of it. God, Jack, it was awful. Did I do the right thing, did I?'

I wondered then, about doing the right thing. It seemed like sometimes when you did what you thought was the right thing, you turned around and suddenly it wasn't the right thing at all. That hindsight thing again. I wondered why Mo had been so keen to see Caroline, why the question about me and Pete, and why did she think Julia might have gone to Australia. Caroline said she had the same questions. She said that Mo had been really agitated, and what was odd was that she'd asked if Julia had said anything about her and Julia, as if she was worried about the two of them. I said that I thought they must have had some kind of argument, something like that. I didn't put it past Julia to argue with anyone. She could have argued with a saint, made the saint out to be the devil and left the saint wondering if it should switch sides. Caroline laughed at this, and we cuddled up on her sofa together. I felt better, stronger. Caroline was like oxygen to me, like my life blood, my energy giver, my sanity, my saint, my angel.

So, Mo thought Julia had gone to Australia. Well, well. Caroline and I agreed it made things easier. Caroline was still for us – us mind - telling the police, and said as much. But it could work out. We could simply let Mo believe Julia had gone to be with Pete, and if they'd had a row, then it would make sense that Julia would not want any communication. It seemed too good to be true. Caroline rightly said that as an only daughter, Mo wouldn't maybe put up with that, that she'd try to find her. I thought that was all right, though, because she'd no idea who this Pete was or where he was really. She'd have to really want to find her, and that would take time, and we needed time. Caroline said I wasn't to worry about Bob, that the compost plan was fine so long as I barrowed it up and took it to him. She did say, though, that I should tell the police. She said she'd go with me, that we should come clean about it all. And I think she was right, that would be the best thing. But things had gone a bit far, and if we could sort the Mo thing, we'd be home and dry. I still had the stuff to sort with Julia's bank and things like that, but that was okay. Mind, if stuff wasn't drawn out, if there was no activity in her account and such, it would add to the case that she'd disappeared and not gone to Australia at all. The police could check stuff like that, never mind data protection, they had powers. I didn't want to think about it, though, it was too much. I would need to add it to the list. The list was in my pocket. It was always in my pocket. I fished it out and showed it to Caroline. It was a bit crumpled, and I probably needed to write out a new list, but it looked like this,

- Post
- ~~Julia coming home – prepare for ALL~~
- Coffee table/Overbury Hall
- ~~My Will – to be cremated.~~
- A or T
- Failure - talk to C

Caroline asked me about failure but I couldn't talk to her about it really, because I felt such a failure. She didn't press me, and instead said I could talk when I was ready, when I wanted to. It wasn't that I didn't want to, I just didn't know how really, how to tell the woman I loved that the woman I had been married to all those years had made me feel a complete failure, a sexual incompetent. Inadequate. I was a failure. Failed marriage, no children, no future – or at least not until now – failed sex life, inadequate husband. Caroline listened to me, and poured me another drink. I reeled it all off, it wasn't easy, and it came in fits and starts. I couldn't tell her it all, she'd wonder what the hell she was doing with me if I did. But I told her enough to hopefully get across what failure meant. She understood. She said it was only natural I should have those feelings, after all I'd been through, and that I should try to accept them. I wondered about that, that I was really angry about what had happened. I told her about punching the lounge cushions. She said that was natural too, and reminded me that there was nothing wrong with our sex life. She made me feel a whole lot better, but I couldn't help being angry, and couldn't see how it was natural – none of this was natural to me. Mind, Caro was talking about the feelings, not the situation, she did say that to me. She said the situation was really bizarre. That was the word, bizarre.

25. *Mo goes to Australia again*

Mo was annoyed with herself. She'd been all the way over to Caroline's and had not got much further in finding out about Pete and Julia. It was obvious to her that Caroline knew more about the whole thing than she was letting on. She was so tight lipped which could only mean that Julia had clearly given her instructions on what to say. Mo reckoned that Julia had gone with Pete, or followed him to Australia, and if she had, she would find them and this wouldn't be difficult, as Pete's company address would be on the net somewhere. He'd told her a bit about his work and the area in Australia where he lived, so she could track him down and she was sure to find Julia there, though God alone knows why. Pete must have told her about them and spun her some sort of line, she reasoned, and that was why Julia wasn't talking to her, and she'd got Jack and Caroline on her side. Julia must have told them, which explained why they were being so off with her. God, it was embarrassing for her to think that they all knew about her and Pete. Julia was her only child, and she wasn't going to let that bloody lizard of a man take her away for good. Mo recalled that Julia had been a complicated child, and now she was a complicated woman who seemed to have a thing for men who weren't good for her, in fact she always had, except for Jack who'd been solid - gullible, but solid.

It had been a relief to Mo when, all those years ago, Julia had announced she and Jack were getting married, as she and Julia had not been getting on at all, with argument after argument about everything and nothing, mostly about the men Julia was going around with, or staying out with, until all hours of the night and early morning. To be honest, Mo was happy to see her married and gone from the house, even if it was to Jack. Back then, she didn't know him from Adam and let's face it, she still didn't know him very well and he and Julia had been married for years, and just exactly how they'd stayed married was a mystery to Mo because Jack kept himself to himself, and he didn't exactly encourage conversation, he and Julia didn't seem to have anything in common, and they didn't seem to do very much together either.

The thought suddenly struck her, then, that she could check with Jack about Julia and Pete, she could get him to tell her if Julia had gone with Pete to Australia or not. He would tell her, or at least he wouldn't be able to hide it from her if she confronted him face to face. She was sure he knew about Pete, and he knew about Julia and Pete, husband or not, so she drove off to her daughter's house to get what she wanted out of Jack. It never occurred to her that the husband might feel a little bit uncomfortable talking about his wife's infidelity in front of his mother in law. She was a woman on a mission, she knew what she wanted and she was going to damned well get it.

She arrived at Julia's just in time to see Bob wheeling his wheel barrow up the lane, and Mo vaguely recognised him. She drove into the drive, parked the car, and he walked up to her, whistling as he came, then parked the wheel barrow beside her car.

'Alright missus,' he said,

'If you're after Jack Carver, you're early or late and so am I, coz he's not in, if he was in, his car would be here.'

Mo replied,

'It's alright, I'll wait, I'm his mother-in-law.'

'So you are,' said Bob, 'Sorry, I didn't recognise you. We have met, I think, a while back.'

'That's right, I think I remember, and you are……..?'

'Sorry, um, rude of me, yeah, um, I'm Bob Gwilliam – like William but with a 'G', like 'you get more 'G' when you use me' sort of thing. I'm a builder, sort of, thing, like.'

Bob had held out his hand to shake hers, and stopped then, as she just looked at it. From the look on her face he realised he'd said a bit too much, also, his hand was filthy from digging the soil in Di's patch next door. He pulled it back, wiped it on the backside of his trousers, and then tried to put it away somewhere, but hands on the ends of arms weren't that easy to hide so he folded his arms, and wondered what he should do next. This was a bit awkward for Bob as this was the bloody woman's mother. He'd come to get some compost, but had expected Jack to be there, not that it mattered, as he could probably help himself to the compost and he was sure Jack wouldn't mind, but he still felt like he'd been caught out at something.

She said,

'I see. Well, it's clear he's not here then, but my daughter might be, that's her car.'

She pointed to the silver-grey fiat Punto, and continued,

'I'm her mother, Maureen Pritchard.'

Bob had realised who it was, as he remembered he had met her once or twice before, the first time was at Jack's wedding yonks ago, and he'd met her again but he couldn't recall when or where. She was a good looking woman, he thought, that's where Jules got it from, a bit skinny but good for her age, and she obviously looked after herself, mind she looked like she might have the money to do it. It was odd to him to meet Jack's mother in law, mother of the sodding woman who had seduced him and then blackmailed him into sodding well lying. He wondered if Julia had got all that from her mother, was Julia the only first rate bitch in the family, or were there two?

Bob said,

'Oh, that's nothing, the car's been there not moved for a while, I wouldn't bank on her being here because of that if I were you. Have you tried the bell?'

'No, I've only just arrived this minute as you know, and since I've arrived you have been talking to me, so how can I have?' She seemed irritated.

'Sorry,' said Bob.

She looked him up and down, and asked,

'Are you the gardener?'

'Me, um, well.........'

It occurred to Bob that he could say yes to this, and just get on and get the compost - which he was itching to do - and let the woman think he was the gardener as that was clearly all she thought he was, but he thought better of it. Jack might arrive any minute and then where would that leave him? Something from school about webs and deception came into his head, and he didn't want to get all tangled up in stuff like that again. He'd had enough of that with Julia, so he thought better of it. He said,

'No, I'm a mate of Jack's, well, of him and um, well, of Jack's really, I um, I live, no I'm doing some work next door, for a friend, Jack's neighbour, like, in her garden. Shall we ring the bell, knock just in case? He leaves it open round the back sometimes if he's not going to be long, you could wait, I'm not sure where he is just now mind, you could leave a note or summit. I could pass on a message if you like, like.'

They both went round the back, and the back door was open, so Mo decided to wait. Bob thought better of getting the compost with her around, and didn't want to wait with Mo, so went back next door to Di's, but before he went, he moved the empty wheel barrow from the front drive to next to Jack's compost heap, ready. There was a strange smell there, very strange, one that was familiar to Bob, though he couldn't quite place it. He knew that smell. It was an animal smell, the smell of decay, as if some animal had died there. He must mention it to Jack.

It felt very strange for Mo to be in her daughter's house alone. She'd not been there very much at all, Julia hadn't really wanted her to. The house seemed very empty and she didn't want to snoop around too much, but she couldn't resist looking round the ground floor to see if anything had changed, and it was all as she remembered it. They'd had the conservatory built, of course, so that had changed things a bit, but it was all still the same everywhere else. Julia wasn't at all what you would call a house proud woman, she spent all her energy on the horses and did precious little around the house which could do with a damned good dust and hoover round, thought Mo, running her finger across the top of a side table. Typical Julia. She was surprised that they didn't have a cleaner in, but then Jack probably didn't approve of that sort of thing, too mean probably, or maybe his sort didn't have cleaners. She wondered about upstairs, if they had separate rooms, which she'd always suspected but never asked, and Julia had never talked about it. She stood at the bottom of the stairs and looked up, wondering about whether to go up or not. Then, she heard a car drive up outside.

Jack and Caroline got out of Jack's car. They'd decided to get back to Jack's place, and when they arrived they'd seen the strange car on the driveway. Jack unlocked the front door and they went in. They heard a voice, which they both recognised as Mo's voice, saying,

'Hello, Jack is that you?'

And then there she was, right in front of them. She saw them both together. She said, in a surprised sort of voice,

'Jack, I hope you don't.......oh, Caroline, it's you as well!'

She didn't even have the decency to look uncomfortable, sort of pointed her nose upward a bit, and explained about how it had come about that she was in the house, about meeting Bob - that was his name - the gardener, and he'd shown her around to the back and said it was all right if she waited.

Jack made them all a drink and they sat in the conservatory, overlooking the garden in the sort of uneasy making the usual small talk, when people have got something to say but say anything but the thing they need to say. Mo looked at Caroline, and then at Jack and she asked Jack if she could have a word, privately, to which Jack said anything she needed to say, she could say in front of Caroline. Caroline wasn't too sure about this and offered to leave, but Jack insisted that she stay. Caroline was thinking about the compost heap, and Julia, and that she'd had the television on at home before Jack had arrived, sort of in the background, and had heard that they'd discovered the body of a woman. She'd rushed into the living room convinced that it must be about Julia, but realised with relief that it wasn't. The strange thing, the funny thing was, as she said to Jack after he'd he turned up, was that she'd somehow got the subtitles on screen, and instead of saying they'd discovered a 'body, it said they'd discovered a 'balti'. It wasn't funny really, but somehow it was.

So, the three of them were all politeness, with an undercurrent that hinted that they were far from polite, and far from comfortable and Caroline wished she was anywhere but where she was. To her, Jack seemed cool, aloof, and focussed, while into her head on and off she mulled over how much of a deep thinker he was, and how a lot went on with him that he never showed on the outside, so this coolness was not real and to her, he was like one of those deep pools at the foot of a waterfall, into which torrents of water could fall and be absorbed, ice cold, and unchanged over the years despite the crashing of water onto its surface and into its depths. He was an ice pool that she could dive into and happily drown in, and, with an ice-cold, instant and uncontrollable reflex, the water would be sucked into her lungs, and she would sink into the dark of his deepness forever. She felt she could die in him.

Caroline heard Mo take in a deep breath. Mo seemed to steel herself, steady herself, and then she spoke. She said she knew all about Julia, and Pete, and it looked to her like Jack and Caroline were an item, that she wasn't born yesterday, that was obvious what was going on, and she didn't blame Jack exactly because she knew things weren't good between him and Julia – so that was by the by. She said she suspected Julia had gone to Australia to be with Pete to spite her for reasons she wasn't going to go into, and that wasn't it best that they both just come clean and tell her what was going on, because she knew they damned well knew, and she wasn't going to go away until she had found out where Julia was. She stopped then, and took a breath, and carried on that if she had to she would bloody well go to Australia after Julia to set her straight if that's what it took, because she wasn't going to have some sex mad perverted bloody Aussie poisoning her only daughter towards her, and did they know that he was actually from Sutton Coldfield, and not Australia at all, nothing bloody glam about that, nor was being a geologist or miner or whatever, so what had they both got to say?

26. Confession time

I wondered when we saw the car, whose it was, but never twigged that it might be Mo's. I hadn't expected her to just turn up, and how she got in the house was a mystery but she soon cleared that up. I'd have to have a word with Bob. Fancy showing her in, and then what had possessed him to leave her alone in the house? She could have looked at anything, snooped round and stuff, I wouldn't put it past her. Bloody woman. I didn't trust her one little bit, and I didn't like her being in the house. Even Julia hadn't much cared to have her visit the house, she was always careful to meet up with her somewhere else, or go over to her house. Even so, I couldn't just ask her to leave. And there was Caroline, with me. Mo was bound to put two and two together when she saw us together. I was right about that. She twigged right off. When she started talking, I wasn't sure where she was going, but she really didn't have a clue. She thought Julia had gone with Pete to Australia, but I didn't get the thing about it being to spite her. Caroline sat quietly, calmly. She was brilliant at listening. She and I, we both sat and listened to Mo, without interrupting – not that she gave much opportunity. When she stopped, I wasn't sure what to say, I looked at Caroline, and she at me. I thought it should be me that should say something. I was the one that had put her daughter in the – no, I couldn't think of that right now – she needed an answer, and she was already at the answer I'd wanted her to have. She'd done our work for us really, the thing Caroline and I had talked about, about Julia going to Australia. Mo believed it, for some reason, she thought that's what had happened. So why not let her believe it? After all, it wouldn't be lying, exactly, just letting Mo believe what she wanted to believe. That was very different. I just wouldn't correct her, that was all. What was wrong with that? All this truth business can hurt, I thought, people set too much store by it, Sometimes it was kinder to let people live happy in a lie, than unhappy with the truth – wasn't it? It seemed to make sense to me, that there was no need for the big confession. If she knew Julia was dead she would be really hurt. She could ring Pete, of course, if she could track him down. And he'd tell her Julia wasn't there. She may not believe him, mind. If she went to Australia and found Pete, she'd learn that Julia wasn't there soon enough and where would that leave her? With a missing daughter. We could claim ignorance, maybe. The police would get involved, that was probably inevitable. I'd have to think about that. Mo said,

'What have you both got to say then, on that score?'

The brain was an amazing thing, to be able to think all this stuff in fractions of seconds, like a sort of thought-tardis, pretty small from the outside but masses of huge things going on, on the inside in a really short space of time – and you can't even see it working.

My brain was working overtime then, trying to figure out what to say to Mo but Caroline got there before me.

'What do you mean, she might have done it to spite you? Why would she do that?'

'Because, well, it's personal. I don't need to tell you about that. It's just something between Julia and myself, all right, something personal.'

Mo looked really unhappy, she fiddled with her mug, and continued,

'Look, I've got to speak to her. There are things she needs to know, from me. Point of fact, she's not answering her phone, she's not here, she's not anywhere. Her car is here, but she's not. Aren't you at all worried? She seems to have disappeared, and I think I know why, and where maybe, but I don't really know, and I have to see her, speak to her. I just want you to tell me what you know. Tell me where she is, and I'll go. Caroline, are you sure she didn't say anything on holiday? Did she, did she mention anything about me and………well, anything on that score?'

I looked at Caroline, I could see she wasn't happy at all. Caroline replied,

'No, she didn't say anything on holiday, and, well, to be honest, we sort of fell out, y'know.'

I couldn't stand any more of it, I said,

'Look, Mo. It's been over between me and Julia for a long time. You know that, and I think pretty much everyone knows that. The marriage was a sham from the start really. Julia had been seeing blokes, I've no idea how many and she saw some more often than others – including this Pete guy. So she might have been planning to go off with him, how the hell would we know? She never said a word. She's a grown up woman and she can do what she likes. She's been a bloody nightmare, sorry to say that to you, as you're her mother, but that's how it was. Sorry.'

So, I wasn't exactly lying. Not exactly. Caroline told Mo that she'd been doing Julia's horses and not to worry about those. Mo asked if we had any contact details for Pete in Australia, but neither of us did. She said she would try to find him, that it shouldn't be too difficult, that he had a mobile, and she would track him down if he didn't return her calls. I wondered how come it was that she knew he had a mobile and why would she have his mobile number but she seemed to be talking on auto pilot, as if she was planning out what she was going to do by saying it out loud to us, that somehow by saying it out loud, it would all happen. She said she would let us know if she found out anything, that she'd possibly end up going to Australia, that she had some friends in Perth so it wouldn't be an altogether wasted trip, come to that, to let her know immediately if we heard anything. I said it was not likely, but that of course we would if we did. That bit at least was true. Then she got up to leave, and I felt a bit sorry for her then, and a bit of a bastard in that she didn't know about Julia being here, dead, in the compost, and that I was the one that put her there, and was not telling her the whereabouts of her dead daughter. Some son in law. She never thought much of me, and once she knew, it would confirm her view that she'd been right all along. Bastard.

As I showed her out, there was a waft of a breeze and I caught a strange smell, sort of sickly sweet but not pleasant. I noticed the wheel barrow, Bob's wheel barrow, by the compost heap. Shit. What the hell was that doing there? Had Bob helped himself while I was out? Had he found anything? That smell, he was sure to have noticed it. I had the bird-choke feeling in my throat again. I didn't wait for Mo to drive away, as soon as she was in the car, I ran back in to the house. Caroline looked at me, she had a worried look on her face. She said,

'Jack, there's something not right here. What's gone on with Mo and Julia do you think? And, why has Mo got Pete's mobile number? What's that all about? God, Jack, we can't keep this up, we need to go to the police, let's go and tell them what's happened. Come on, shall we?'

I couldn't. I just couldn't. I told her about the smell and Bob's wheel barrow.

'You see,' she said.

'We can't stop the smell, can we. And what if he's found her? He'll not keep quiet will he? He can't keep his mouth shut about anything. And, he knows quite a bit about Pete as well, doesn't he? Jack, we can't keep this quiet, it's all going to come out, don't you see?'

I did see, but I couldn't go to the police, not now, or not yet, or maybe not ever. I had to know if Bob had found anything. There was a knock at the back door, followed by the door opening, and whistling, then a shout.

'Ay ay! Anyone in? Jack, you in?'

It was Bob. Cheerful as usual. That told me that he couldn't have found Julia wrapped in the carpet.

'Oh, sorry,' he said as he came into the kitchen,

'Not interrupting am I?' He looked at us.

'Someone died or what? You two look as grim as all get out. What's up? Mother in law laying down the law is she? And talk about something dying, I think summat's up and croaked in the garden somewhere, Jack mate 'cause it pongs something rotten. Must be a couple of dog foxes or something like.'

I told Bob what had happened with Mo while he helped himself to a beer from the fridge, and got me and Caroline one as well. He continued,

'Bloody mothers in law, eh, nightmare. Well, I dunno, maybe she'd given Pete a warning off, like, y'know, like stay away from my daughter kind of thing, and he ignored her, and Julia ignored her. They maybe had a row over it. I had a run in with Susie's Mum a bit like that once, and with Julia as well, mind, don't forget, so Mo and I would have that in common. Wouldn't surprise me if she'd taken it into her head to run off with that Pete bloke to Australia. She wasn't well liked here, not that it seemed to make any difference, eh? She seemed to like pissing people off. So, good riddance, that's what I say. Anyhow,'

he changed the subject,

'Onto more important things, Jack, mate, can I, um, have some more compost? Only I didn't like to get any, see, with her ladyship being here, and she thought I was the bloody gardener, bloody cheek of it, me – the gardener! I ask you!'

Bob's theory on the mobile was Mo snooping. She could easily have snooped around Julia's things and found his number. Maybe so. That was the cue for me to let him know I was none too pleased that he'd left her in my house on her own. He said he was sorry about that, but hadn't known what else to do. I guessed that was fair enough. I was just relieved as hell that he hadn't touched the compost.

He went next door then, and I barrowed him a few loads round, plenty to keep him going. Then I got back to the house, and took a shower. No amount of water would wash it all away, though. Caroline was brilliant. She knocked us up something to eat, and we opened a bottle. She said we needed to talk about going to the police. I knew she was right. It seemed to me that she was always right about stuff. She had a way of putting it that made it seem like the right thing. Why hadn't I just come clean and told the police at the start? It was too late now, that was what kept going through my head. I'd be guilty of killing Julia, for the affair with her best friend. No jury would believe it had started up afterwards. And would we be able to get Pete back from Australia to testify? Would he be for or against me? Mo would have my balls for breakfast, that's for sure. Then Caroline said something interesting, something that I think not even she had pieced together fully. It came out as a question, then and we both looked at each other and realised something. Something we'd not realised before. She said,

'You know Jack, Bob said he had a run in with Julia. When do you think that was?'

I didn't know. Caroline said,

'Well, what if it was just before the so-called Turkey holiday? And Pete, he said he'd had a row with her as well, didn't he? An argument or whatever, I forget what he said exactly, but what if,

Jack, what if they'd been in the house that day, Bob and Pete? What if there'd been some kind of row and one of them had knocked her down and killed her, and not you at all? Pete was mightily relieved when he found out she'd gone to Turkey, more than someone would be normally, I think. What do you think? Jack?'

I was thinking. So it might not have been me at all. It couldn't have been Bob, he wouldn't hurt a fly. Pete, now, Pete was another matter altogether. But surely I'd know if there was someone else in the house? Caro said,

'No, you wouldn't why would you? You were in the workshop, what with all the noise and that. Do you remember what you were doing in there? Was it noisy?'

I didn't remember really, in the spray booth, I thought. Anyway the workshop was away from the house, and the door faced up the garden with no view to the drive, so I wouldn't have seen a strange car or heard anything. Caroline could be right. There could have been someone else in the house. It might not have been me that killed Julia after all. Not Bob, but Pete, yes, it could have been. Caroline said something else then, something that I didn't realise had happened. She said,

'Jack, actually, Julia and I had a fight that day I think, it's hard to remember exactly what day it was, but I'm sure it was that day. She'd been going on about Pete and how she'd strung him along, how he was a good fuck, and how gullible men were, you in particular. I lost it, Jack, I, well, I told her I couldn't stand the way she was treating you, that she didn't know how lucky she was to have you and she should maybe think about making the marriage work. She laughed, she just laughed in my face, and I was so angry, Jack, God forgive me, but I lashed out, I slapped her across the face. I think I hit her quite hard, actually but I didn't mean to. It just happened.' She continued,

'Julia and I well, you know we were once very close, at school, inseparable, like sisters we were. She had such a hard time at home, she had no one, really, only me, and I only had her. We were a bit wild, I know, we both liked going out, we liked dating, liked being taken out, and we were both passionate about horses. She was the one who did something about that, I so admired her then, that she got the business together and that, and it sort of kept us together as friends I guess. But she got worse, with men, I mean, while I......I guess I grew out of it. I thought I could help her, set her straight but she just.......she just got worse. She had a string of boyfriends – sorry Jack, this was before you came along – and I thought if I was there for her to talk to, she would be okay. But she wasn't. I was a fool, really, to think I could influence her. I just had this thought, believed if you like, that the friend I knew, the Julia I knew, all those years ago, was in there somewhere and would reappear given time. I thought she'd, I dunno, grow out of it or something, like me, that the wildness would calm down. I was wrong. It had gone too far with her. She hated men – really hated them. She had this thing that she was going to get revenge for what had happened to her, for what her Dad did to her when she was growing up. I didn't really see it properly until Pete came back this last time. She needed help, Jack, proper help. Psychological help. I wasn't helping her. I realise now that I never could. Some friend, eh?'

I didn't know what to say to her. I'd never thought of Julia as a basket case, or anyone's friend really, although strangely I'd always known that Caroline was her friend. It all made sense though. I was quiet, thinking about it. Caroline hated me being quiet. She said,

'Well, say something. I didn't mean to blow up with Julia, I know I should have kept my cool but I just couldn't help it, I was so furious with her. You do know I've never done anything like that before, don't you, please Jack, say something, say it's all right, she was all right when I left her, I know that. Please, Jack, say you forgive me, please?'

Of course I forgave her, in fact there was nothing to forgive. She wasn't the one who'd done it. I was glad she'd told me. I took her in my arms and held her to me, and we were both quiet then, thinking our own thoughts for a while.

That smell I'd smelled outside seemed to still be with me, it had stuck in my nose, and I could smell it still. I didn't know that smell but still I recognised it. It was the smell of decay – Julia's decay – and if I had noticed it, others would too.

27. Contact

'Hello?'

'Yes?'

'Is that Pete?'

'Who's asking?'

'Mo.'

'Mo? G'day luv, long time. What's up?'

'Pete, listen, I have to know if Julia's with you.'

'Why the hell would she be with me?'

Mo answered,

'Because, because of you and me, and she..... well you know damned well why. You told her didn't you?'

'Well, that's as may be, but she ain't here luv, so there's not much for us to talk about, Mo. Best we leave it there, eh?'

Pete made it sound final.

'Just tell me where she is, please," Mo continued,

"Tell her I want to talk to her, can't you even do that you bastard? Is she with you?'

'Look Mo, no need for the strong language, luv, we had a good time, me and Julia too. But let's leave it there. I dunno where she is, and if I did I'm not sure I'd be wanting to get all involved in this whatever, mother and daughter thing. It's not my thing, okay?

I've got better things to be doing. Best you don't call me again, luv, and if you do, I'll just get my service to block any calls from you. Sorry to be so blunt, like Mo, but that's how it is y'know. Anyhow, bit busy right now, so best say g'bye. G'bye Mo.'

And Pete ended the call. Mo was furious. Dammit she was sure Julia was out there with him, the bastard, and that Julia had got him on her side. Why the hell did she want him? He was a complete bastard. There was nothing for it. She'd contact her friends in Perth, and she'd go out there and see what she could find out, she wasn't about to let this Pete come between her and Julia. She and her daughter hadn't had the best of relationships, that was certain, but Julia was her only child and she wasn't about to let her just disappear somewhere in the wilds of Australia thinking her mother was a complete bitch.

Pete worked for a mine, Mo knew that, somewhere a long way from Perth because he'd said to her he'd had to fly across to Perth for business now and again. If she could only remember what the mine was called. Mo remembered it was something Scottish sounding, Argyll or Ardesh, no, dammit she just couldn't remember. Still, diamond mines couldn't be that obscure, she'd look on the web and see if that jogged her memory. She poured herself a large gin and tonic and switched on the computer. She wasn't the best at computers but she did know how to look for things, shopping mostly. And there it was, Arbroath Mine, in the northern part of Western Australia. That's where he'd be, and that's where Julia would be. She hadn't any idea about Australia, and hadn't realised just how beautiful it was. This part was really rugged, and mountainous, with what looked like a fabulous lake. Her friends Glynnis and Tim had gone out to live in Perth after their son emigrated three years before. He was their only son, and he'd got married to an Australian girl, then had two children. They were determined to be close to their grandchildren, and decided to leave England and live in Perth permanently. It hadn't been easy, and had taken over a year to make happen. They'd bored Julia rigid with all the plans and paperwork and visa stuff – and photos of the trips back and forth of places and the grandchildren. To say she was bored wasn't quite right. She was envious. Envious of their marriage, and envious of their son who seemed to love them to bits. She was envious of the letters and photos, and of their seemingly saintly daughter in law – whatever her name was – and of their grandchildren, all of whom could walk on water and perform a range of other miraculous activities including talking and walking. She envied them that they had grandchildren at all, and that the children seemed so perfect in every way. It was like those circular letters she got each year from a couple of old friends, that went on about how great everything was, the hiking trips across Vietnam, that son number two had got a first at Cambridge and had been hand-picked to become a top government something or other, another passing law exams and set to be a top barrister. Nothing like her life. What would she say to people she'd not seen in thirty years? Hello! Sorry not to have been in touch been living life to the full, of course, and too busy to write, in that regard, but husband died a while back after a solo trip to Thailand, and that wasn't easy to pull off even with our huge financial portfolio (mind, that was about the only huge thing about him). How good for him to have had that last holiday, and what a shame he never came round after the heart attack so that he could tell us all about it, but we did see the photos, which the police now have, otherwise like you, we'd have made our own Christmas cards with one of them on the front. His treatment for impotence never quite worked, but he didn't let this interfere with getting on with things. His hobby, for example, took him to various parts of Europe and the Far East, always on his own. Julia, our only daughter (there was a brief episode when his pipework and our marriage was in working order) has been happily married for some time, to someone I hardly know. She is so happily married that she insists on sharing her happiness with other people – mostly men – at all times of the day and night, and has been generous enough to share one of her friends with her mother. Oh, and she runs a very successful equine supplies business – you might have heard of it 'Equine Essentials', an

Aladdin's cave of bridles and leather wear to suit all pockets, a choice of brand names, hand-made fully adjustable saddles and a saddle fitting service, high performance bedding and an extensive range of bits. We must meet, up soon....

Yes, that would about do it. Not too much of the confessional. If she was going to be confessional, how about how she had failed her daughter, failed to stand up to a bully, paedophile, and a liar. It all seemed to make sense looking back, but she'd done nothing at the time. She thought she'd been in a kind of paralysis, something like a suspended animation. She couldn't blame post-natal depression, not for all of it as it wasn't even known about then really, but she was sure that's what it was, or at least that was the start of it all.

'Pull yourself together', her mother had said, so she pulled herself together on the outside, and pulled herself apart on the inside and stayed that way for years. She still wasn't really back together but she made a good show of it on the outside. Maybe that was why there was that joke about the person that goes to the doctor, claiming he think he's a pair of curtains, and the doctor says, 'Pull yourself together.'

She'd drawn her curtains across herself so tight so no chink of light could get in and no one could see inside to the bloody and battered pieces of her broken self scattered all over. It was maybe living with him that did it. Why hadn't she done something? Why had she refused to believe what was going on, and to her own daughter? Why hadn't she left him, gone to the police? It had all seemed so unreal at the time, she hadn't been sure of anything. She remembered how he had called her 'mad and sad', said that no one would believe her, that they were sure to take Julia into care and put her away too, and he'd sign the paper. He called her a 'sad, raving mad, bitch'. She'd been a fool to believe him. Bloody heart attack was too easy a death really.

And now this. This thing with Pete. She was sure Julia blamed her for what happened. Maybe she could put a bit of that in when she talked to Glynnis and Tim. It would scare the shit out of them, all of them, all the ones who thought her life was full of shopping and coffee mornings and she wondered if all the people she knew, she could hardly call them friends, who seemed to be happy, in fact had sad and twisted lives of their own. She doubted it, but how would she know? It wasn't something you could just come out and ask about, and maybe, just maybe, everyone had their own kind of curtains. She wondered what they thought about her life. She had always thought that bringing up Julia and keeping the house was her main job, that it was enough. Julia's father hadn't wanted her to work, but she'd wanted to, so she'd got a job as a secretary at the local cider firm when she met him, but then they were taken over, she'd been made redundant, and then

Julia had come along, amazingly. That was the end of the paid work, and her independence, after which nothing seemed the same. Funny how money seemed to come into it after that, having to ask him for money for everything, which meant she was totally dependent on him, and he was in control and he bloody well showed it. He knew where to hit her so the bruises wouldn't show, clever bastard that he was.

But that was then, and this was now and she had to get to Julia. She got on the web and booked herself on a return flight to Perth. She checked the time, and rang Glynnis, who was delighted to hear from her, long time no see and all that, and in between speaking she was shouting other things to people Mo couldn't see or hear, like,

'Tim, Tim, it's Mo, remember? Mo from back home, y'know? Della, Dell, it's Mo, you remember Mo? Oh, you never met her, of course, sorry love, did he want something with that? It's only regurg, not real sick.'

Then she was back to Mo, saying how great it was that she would be coming to Perth, what flight was she on, and of course they'd meet her, and Perth was to die for, there was so much so see and she must let them show her the sights, and little Bobbie was four now and so clever – could she believe it, wasn't that just amazing?

The flight was the next day, and when she'd made the booking they'd told her how to get an electronic visa. This left her time to find out a bit more about the Arbroath mine - Kimberley, that was where it was and it would be easy to get a flight out there when she got to Perth. She packed and got ready, took a look at her mobile, but there was still nothing from Julia. She wasn't really expecting her to call or text, and Mo wasn't sure if her mobile would work out there, but she sent Julia a text anyway.

Can explain all. Please call me. Please. Am coming to you, know you are with him. It's all ok. Do love you. Am sorry. Mum xx

28. Uncovering

I suppose I never thought about friends, really, What friends were, or meant, or anything like that. They just were. Bob just was. But here was the thing. He'd found out about Julia, about her not being alive. He found her being dead. And I realised what friendship was. Funny how it is that you can know someone for a long time, years, and not know them. Or you think you know them, but you don't really. You only know when the shit hits the fan, then you know. Like when Bob turned up in the kitchen with Di, and his face was all kind of grey and serious. He had lines on his face that I'd not noticed before. He looked older. He was not one to be serious usually, but he said,

'Jack, um Jack, me and Di, well me, I think you should know that we found something. In the compost. Something, well, er, somebody.'

I heard the emphasis in his voice, on the word 'body'.

Caroline was at my side, she took my hand and squeezed it.

Bob told us that he had been in the garden, in my garden. He'd decided to help himself to some compost, thinking it would do no harm in particular as I'd given him some already, and what did a couple more barrow loads matter. I felt that sick feeling again, the bird in the throat thing, as if it was in there, stuck tight and struggling in my throat. The compost, I thought, Well, I couldn't begrudge him that, I'd have done the same. I couldn't speak, felt frozen, sort of paralysed. Everything in me felt heavy, and distant, unreal.

Bob went on how he had got one load of compost, and noticed a really horrible smell, but thought it might be a dead fox. And when he came back for a second load he shoved in the spade and the spade hit something, and something sort of fell out. A foot. A person's foot. He didn't know whose foot, of course, but it was a foot all the same, with painted toe nails, a woman's foot. He described how he had puked up in the bush next to the compost heap - we could have done without that bit - and he said how he'd then gone straight to Di and she hadn't believed him but she'd gone and looked. Di stared at me. She said that as soon as Bob had told her, she had put two and two together, that it must be Julia, and it couldn't be anyone else. She looked me straight in the eyes, and said,

'Well, Jack, is it? Is it Julia? Did you do, well, you know, did you? Did you put her in the compost heap? Jack, is it her?'

What could I say? I looked at Bob, and Dianne, then at Caroline, and she looked straight back at me, and nodded. Her gaze was clear and straight, true as a die. I wished she would say something, anything, but she was quiet, I said,

'Well, Bob, you know, um. well, this isn't easy, Christ it's bloody hard, but yes, it is Julia. It's her, but it's not what you think, it's not. It's not what you think, Caroline, tell them, please..........'

Straight away Caroline said.

'He didn't do it. It wasn't Jack. He just put her there.'

Bob looked at Di, and then said, to my amazement,

'Jack, I dunno what's happened or anything that made you put her in the compost, but there's something you do need to know, about me and Julia. I'm sorry, mate, I'm not proud of what I did, and I - we - think you should know.'

Di took over then, as Bob sank onto one of the kitchen chairs and put his head in his hands. He was sobbing gently. Di was stood over him, with her arms around his shoulders. I was gob smacked. I couldn't take it in. What the hell was he saying? What more could there be about him and Julia? It didn't make sense. None of it did. Di was a bit more with it than Bob. Caroline had put the kettle on the Aga, to make tea. She said we could all do with some. Dianne said that Bob had told her a while back that he and Julia had had a row, over her blackmailing him to do stuff. Bob had had enough. He'd hit her and she'd fallen backwards, it was more than just the reactive slap that he'd told me about before. He ran out of the room then, out of her bedroom, thinking he should just get away. Bob interrupted then.

'Bloody bitch she was Jack, sorry and all, but Christ she was calling you all sorts of names and threatening to tell you about me and her, and I just lost it. Never hit a woman in my life before, I just lost it, lashed out, God, I'm sorry, I'm so sorry, I never thought………….but she went on holiday, with her mother, with Mo, didn't she – she was all right when I left her wasn't she? Jack – was she? So what happened, what the hell happened to her that you could do that to her?'

He stopped then, unable to carry on. He was sobbing, shoulders heaving, the whole bit. I couldn't work it out. I thought then that maybe, just maybe it was him that had done it. He might have whacked Julia while I was in the workshop. It was just like Caroline had said. It could have been someone else, not me. But he'd discovered her body. He knew it was Julia's – or at least Di had worked that out. They knew she was dead, and that Bob had hit her. But it might not have been Bob. Caroline got there at the same time as me. Pete. I said,

'Look, Bob, Julia never went anywhere. There never was a holiday. We don't know how but she ended up dead that's for sure, I found her, and Chris-sakes I thought it was me, and I put her in the compost. God alone knows what possessed me to do that, I thought no one would miss her really, bitch that she was, but you weren't the only one that hit her. There's that Pete guy she was seeing. He said he'd whacked her and he was really bothered about it, honest. I'm, well, just a bit confused about it all really, I can't make it out, what happened and who saw her when. All I know is I found her, dead, in the bedroom, and I couldn't remember what had happened. I'd no idea that you, well, that you had hit her, but that wouldn't be enough to kill her, Bob. Bob - you do know that don't you?'

Caroline looked at Bob, and me then, and said,

'Actually, you know I did as well. I think it might have been the same day, at least, I think it was the same day. We had a huge row about the way she was treating Jack, and I couldn't go on being her friend. It wasn't a real friendship anyway, we were trading more on what had been once, than what there really was. We'd got less and less in common, anyway, it got a bit, y' know, well we argued. I've never done that before, not to anyone, not ever. It just sort of, well, happened. She looked shocked, sort of fell back, and I stormed out. I didn't think any more of it at the time. I thought I'd ended a friendship, ended something and just look at it now. She's dead, and it might have been me. I might have been the one.'

I reminded her about Pete. Bob said,

'Well it might have been me, God-sakes Jack, it might have been me, and you put her in the compost – what the hell were you thinking, why didn't you go to the rossers? Are you a bloody maniac or what? And I had to, had to find her, I had to find out like that, like…..like that!'

'I don't know. Caroline said just the same to me. Don't you think I haven't asked myself over and over? I just, I dunno, something sort of inside me, I dunno, just seemed like I could make her go away, and then when Caro and I got together I thought it might go badly, that people – the police – might think that I'd done it to be with Caroline. Christ, I don't know, I just don't sodding well know.'

Caroline passed me a cup of tea, one to Bob, and one to Dianne. I went to the sitting room, came back with a bottle of whisky and some glasses, poured one for each of us and drank mine straight off. We all just stood there, in silence. Each trying to get our heads round it I suppose, or at least Di and Bob were, because it wasn't all new to me or Caroline. It was worse for Bob and Di. Di spoke first.

'So, Caroline, you, um, you knew did you? About Julia and stuff, you were in on it were you? What's to say this whole thing wasn't planned, I'm sorry but, what if this was planned by the two of you?'

Caroline was shocked, and replied,

'What? No, Di, Christ, no - whatever you might think, please don't think that. God, no.'

This was the last straw. Me and Caroline, planned the thing, bloody outrageous. I said angrily,

'Look here Di, don't be bloody daft. We'd not do anything like that! What the hell are you thinking? This with me and Caro, it's well, it's only been since…..you know, Not before, I swear it. What sort of man do you think I am that I could do that? And well, to think you could think, Chris-sakes, I dunno, I really don't, it's doing my head in.'

I sank into a chair. Bob said,

'Jack, we've been mates for a long time, and I don't think that about you, really, it's just, well, it's just so unbelievable, all of it. She's dead, and you buried her. I just can't take it all in.'

Caroline told Di that she hadn't known about Julia, she said,

'Not for a while, 'cos like you, I thought Jules had gone away, with her mother, but then I saw her mother, Mo, in Waitrose. Mo thought Julia had been away with me. I didn't realise what had really happened, so I didn't like to say anything to her. I thought at first that maybe Julia had done a runner with Pete, you know, she'd always kept him dangling, like a sort of escape plan or side bet just in case. Then when I told Jack I'd seen Mo, it sort of all came out, he told me what had happened.'

Dianne looked at us all, and took a deep breath.

'I've got something to say then, as well. After I came back from holiday, do you remember Bob, just after I got back?'

Bob nodded.

'I came round looking for Jack, and she was in the kitchen. God she was a bitch. She told me she had you wrapped round her little finger, that you were at her beck and call, and if I thought I'd got you, I had another thing coming. She waltzed off upstairs and I followed her. I was telling her she had to leave you alone, but she just laughed. She laughed, Bob, at you and me, and we've got something really special you and me, and I couldn't help it, I, well, I'm not proud of what I did, but I slapped her across the face. She wasn't expecting that. She staggered backwards and fell against the wardrobe. I heard a noise then, someone's voice, a man's voice – not yours Jack - and got a bit scared it might be one of Julia's blokes - you know one of her blokes sort of thing. I ran into the bathroom and hid in there for a minute or two. When the coast was clear I nipped back down the stairs and back to my house. I thought she was all right, you know, that she maybe just banged herself, just maybe hit herself, fell awkward like. God help me, Bob, I'm so sorry, it was might have been me, not you at all, it might have been me!'

She started crying, and Bob hugged her to him. He was sobbing too. What a bloody nightmare.

There was quiet for a few minutes, then Caroline asked Di,

'Di, well you asked me before, now it's my turn, You aren't trying to cover up for Bob are you, Di?'

'No, no I'm not. I have never hit another person in my life. Bob did tell me about Julia, about hitting her, but I never thought......I thought she was all right, that is, well, you know, not dead, I never thought she was dead so I didn't think I needed to say anything. But now, now it's all different.'

'So,' continued Caroline,

'Any one of us could have done it. We were all there that day, all three of us. We all hit her – except we don't know about you, Jack. You could be the only one that didn't – and let's not forget Pete. What about him? He said he'd argued with Julia, and seemed really relieved when we told him she'd gone away with her mother, didn't he Jack? Jack?'

I was miles away. I didn't want to be dragged back to this conversation. In my head I was over the fields by the brook, on the bridge, with water running away beneath and the small waterfall at my back. Running away. That's what I should do. It was all my fault. If I hadn't buried Julia in the compost none of this would be happening. I'd be the one they'd blame, I was up to my neck in the crap of it all. If I'd simply gone to the police no one else would have had to be dragged in. As it was, Caroline, Bob, and now Dianne, were all in the shit with me. Just then the phone rang. I let it ring. We all looked at it, as if that would make a difference. It rang and none of us picked it up. Not a good time, obviously. The answer phone clicked in. It was the lovely Fiona asking about her fucking coffee table, when would it be ready as she had guests this weekend and could I call her. Bob spoke then, 'Why did you put her in the compost? Why there?'

I replied,

'Dunno, seemed right at the time, I just, look, I can't explain it, just that it seemed like the thing to do, to make her go away, to make it all go away.'

'And what about her mother, how did you explain it to Mo?' Dianne asked,

'Didn't people ask about her, about where she was? What about the business stuff, the horses? It's not possible to make someone go away like that, to just disappear, people would want to know where she was, wouldn't they?'

Strangely, there had been surprisingly little by way of questions, it had been easier than I'd imagined. We all like to think we are vital, important, that people around would be sure to notice if we weren't there but it had been pretty easy up to now, really, except for Mo, and Pete. They were the hardest. But it had been hard to lie and impossible to lie to Caroline. Containing the lies was the worst, like having internal floodgates holding back an impossible-to-hold-back flood. Sooner or later the thing would bust wide open and I sensed that this was the beginning, a large crack signalling the beginning of the end. I would have to tell the police. Caroline had been right. But what to say now, now that Bob and Di were involved? How would we find out which of us had done it? How would the police find out? I could, and should own up, say I did it. That would be the thing. Rather than run away, I should take the blame, after all, I'd found Julia dead, buried her, and lied to cover it all up. It was down to me to do the uncovering.

29. *Saying Goodbye*

Mo handed over her passport, and boarding pass at the check in. All okay. She went into duty free and mooched around for a while but still there had been nothing on the mobile from Julia. When the flight was called, she waited in the holding area and she felt nervous. She'd not heard back from Pete, not that she had expected he'd return her texts. Her friends had been really good, offered to meet her at the other end but even so, she wondered what the hell she was doing. It was a hell of an outlay for what could be a wild goose chase but she had an instinct about this and surely to God Julia would be there, after all, where else could she be? Mo wondered about "missing persons". She'd heard about that, how people reported them to the police so maybe she should do that, and she tugged at a fingernail, her nails were a mess, perfectly fine in most people's book, but not in Mo's. It was noisy in the small waiting area, everyone seemed a bit tetchy, with a few young children, running about, wriggling out of their parents' grip. She never would have travelled with Julia when she was that young, but young parents these days didn't seem to care, they went everywhere with their children wrapped up, or unwrapped, in bundles at the front or back or in great big wheeled pushchair things like the nursery equivalent of a Shogun.

Mo didn't travel much because she didn't much like being close up with other people, that is, ones she didn't know, and most travel involved being quite close to strangers. She felt her personal space invaded somehow and she wondered about the flight, how she would stand it, so close up for all that time, relieved that she'd asked for a window seat so she could look out and try to believe that she was up there in the sky alone. She had her walkman – Julia had bought her an iPod nano but she couldn't get on with it – and a couple of books. She didn't much like the smell of other people, and didn't care for small talk with strangers. All that polite meaningless chitter chatter, she thought it was far better to stay quiet, silence was truly a virtue, as most people never had anything much to say anyway, they just repeated what they'd seen on television, or heard on the radio or read in the news, or repeated what other people had said to them. What was the point in all that? Real conversation, now that was a thing, but there wasn't any real conversation anymore and hairdressers were a kind of hell in that regard. If there was an Olympic sport in meaningless chatter, they would get the gold medal every time, that was for certain.

Mo was relieved when she heard them finally call the flight. She picked up her one small bag and joined the queue, amazed at how big some people's bags were, and how the airline seemed to allow stuff on as hand luggage which might have all sorts of hidden pockets and such. Still, she reasoned, things would show up on x-rays, and there were people and dogs specially trained to find things, on that score, as it was their job, after all. She'd seen them all around the airport, even so she had a vague worry that someone might be, just might be carrying something. It flashed through her mind that she wasn't entirely sure that she cared as she was toward the end of her life but would be really awful for those children though, and their relatives. Mo did want to see Julia one more time though, thinking that it would be odd if this were the end, if she got on this plane, and never got off, this journey being the last one she would ever make. She found herself wondering what Julia would make of that, if she would care, or not. Mo was disturbed to think that Julia might not care, after all, because of the thing with Pete, so she had to find Julia and explain to her how it was. If only she could get her to understand, if she'd only return her calls. Just one call, it might be her last, after all. That was rubbish, and Mo knew it as people flew all the time, and she heard one of the children crying, a real tired cry that meant sleep on the plane, eventually. Mo wondered what she would say to Julia if she phoned, and if it was the last conversation they would ever have, mind, neither of them would know if it was the last, so it would probably be a bit awkward, and about nothing very important. Mo found herself wondering why she'd never talked with Julia about anything that really mattered and when she thought about it, it seemed they had always talked about practical things, surface type things, not deep and meaningful things – but then what was between them that meant anything? They went shopping, had coffee and time just seemed to go by, somehow.

Mo was past the desk, her boarding pass checked, and then she walked down the tunnel towards the plane door. And now, what would she say to Julia if she could, that would be any different? Mo realised it was, of course, impossible to think she could recover in one conversation, a relationship that had worn slowly away over years. Something had eaten away at the two of them, mother and daughter, something had gnawed away from the inside until their bones were become fragile as lace, and one inadvertent touch had crumbled them to dust.

The flight was uneventful, with Mo sleeping most of the way, being far more tired that she'd realised. When they landed, she sensed within herself a kind of relief, and wasn't sure why. She gathered her things, and left the plane, stepping out onto the gangway, felt a bit foolish for all the thoughts she'd had before the flight. She breathed in deeply, and then, suddenly, Mo felt an intense pain in her head, saw the floor rising up in slow motion towards her, and it wasn't true about when you die that suddenly your whole life flashes in front of you, as the only thought that flashed for Mo was how floors don't usually move like that. She reached one hand out in front of her to touch it on its way up, she felt her bag fall heavily from her shoulder, then she felt – nothing.

30. Coming home to roost

Dianne, Bob, Jack and Caroline sat in the kitchen and looked at each other, they'd fallen silent, quietly appraising each other, the only sound was the occasional, gently, slurping of tea. A single crow called from the garden, and out of the window it could be seen perched, fat and black, a single strike of ink on a bare tree branch.

They were all jolted out of the silence by the doorbell, and looked at each other, expecting someone would answer it. Jack, on autopilot, put his mug down, and left the kitchen to answer the door with Caroline following him. Jack opened the door and was met with a sight he had not expected – a policeman and a policewoman stood at the door.

"Mr Carver?" the policewoman asked.

Silence. The policewoman asked again,

"We are looking for Mrs Julia Carver, are you her husband?"

Jack finally managed to stammer out,

"Yes, um, yes, sorry, um that's right, I'm Jack Carver, Julia's my, um, my wife."

The policewoman continued,

"Are you Mrs Carver?" asked the policewoman, seeing Caroline standing behind Jack, and Caroline replied.

"No, um, no, I'm, um, a friend of Jack's, and um Julia's, no I'm not her, I'm a friend."

The policewoman paused, looked at them both somewhat suspiciously, and asked,

"Is your wife at home sir? I am afraid we have some bad news, and we need to speak to your wife urgently. May we come in?"

Jack showed the two police officers into the lounge, and motioned Caroline not to follow, so she went into the kitchen where she told Bob and Dianne.

"Shit!" exclaimed Bob,

"Holy shit. I'm fucked. Police. Rossers. They know. They bloody know."

"Don't be stupid, Bob love," said Dianne, "How could they possibly?"

The three of them sat in the kitchen, not wanting to speak, the unspoken agreement being to stay quiet and strain to hear the conversation in the lounge. After what seemed like an age, the kitchen door opened showing Jack framed in the doorway, and he seemed then to Caroline like a three-quarter felled tree, still upright strong and tall, but just the smallest touch would topple him.

Jack told them that Mo was dead. Apparently, the police had been contacted by the Aussie police, to let them know that Mo had keeled over dead after getting off the plane in Oz, and they'd found that she had some kind of condition, a brain thing, well not a brain thing exactly, well a brain thing as well which was what killed her, a bleed on the brain but there was more. She had a condition of the head, inside her head, which was rare, that Julia had very likely inherited, and this meant she could be at risk of the same thing happening to her as well, the same thing as Mo, and she needed to know."

Jack continued, "They said, it was something called artery malformation, or some such."

Caroline nodded, she understood more than Jack, that it was possible – in fact more than probable – that a fall, even a slight one could have been life threatening.

"I've um, I've said Julia's out shopping, but I can't hold it together, I just can't. Mo's dead, and Julia.... she has – had - this artery brain thing, a head knock could be fatal, that's what they are saying, that we need to let Julia know, and.... I told them that.... I told them she is out for the day, shopping. And now..... now they've gone away."

Jack was shaking.

Caroline took Jack by the hand, looked at him with a long and steady gaze, and then turned to look at Bob and Di. And Bob and

Di looked at each other, and at Jack and Caroline, and it was very quiet then in the kitchen, the only sound was the rain which had started falling steadily, and heavily, washing not quite everything away.

Living with Julia

Lightning Source UK Ltd.
Milton Keynes UK
UKOW05f1928280514

232486UK00016B/348/P